*A
Harlequin
Romance*

WELCOME

TO THE WONDERFUL WORLD

of Harlequin Romances!

Interesting, informative and entertaining,
each Harlequin Romance portrays an appealing
love story. Harlequin Romances take you
to faraway places — places with real people
facing real love situations — and
you become part of their story.

As publishers of Harlequin Romances, we're extremely
proud of our books (we've been publishing
them since 1954). We're proud also that Harlequin
Romances are North America's most-read
paperback romances.

Eight new titles are released every month and are
sold at nearly all book-selling stores across
Canada and the United States.

A free catalogue listing all available Harlequin Romances
can be yours by writing to the

HARLEQUIN READER SERVICE, ·
M.P.O. Box 707, Niagara Falls, N.Y. 14302.
Canadian address: Stratford, Ontario, Canada.

or use order coupon at back of book.

We sincerely hope you enjoy reading
this Harlequin Romance.

Yours truly,

THE PUBLISHERS
   Harlequin Romances

CARNIVAL COAST

by

CHARLOTTE LAMB

HARLEQUIN BOOKS TORONTO
WINNIPEG

Original hard cover edition published in 1973
by Mills & Boon Limited.

© Charlotte Lamb 1973

SNB 373-01751-0

Harlequin edition published January 1974

Printed in Canada

1751

CHAPTER ONE

CLAIRE walked out of the cool shadows of the railway station and stood blinking up into skies of incredible, dazzling blue, with an expression of excited surprise. It seemed impossible that it was only yesterday that she had left England, in a grey haze of rain, watching from the ferry as the white cliffs faded rapidly behind their curtain of concealing mist.

This was another world. Palm trees lined the narrow white streets, their exotic shapes outlined against pastel-washed little houses whose pinks, blues and yellows had faded under the impact of the sun. Gay, rainbow blinds protected the customers who were sipping *sirop* at the pavement café opposite. The very shops were unfamiliar and alluring—a baker's window displayed sticks of bread, tumbled baskets of croissants, rich chocolate gateaux, there were excitingly different vegetables and fruit at the stall beside it, and French newspapers outside the little tobacconist's.

"Miss Stratton?"

She turned, startled out of her absorption yet relieved to be met. She had not known whether someone would be waiting at her journey's end. Her telegram had given the time of arrival of her train, of course, but there had not been time to wait for a reply.

She was surprised to see that the man who had approached her was a uniformed chauffeur, but presumably Monsieur Treboul had ordered a hired car to meet her.

"I am Miss Stratton," she said, smiling. "Monsieur Treboul sent you?"

"I am to drive you to the Hotel St. Hilaire, *mademoiselle*," the man replied in strongly accented English.

Claire flushed, bending her head, then allowed him to help her into the back of the sleek grey limousine which was waiting at the kerb. Within moments they were moving through the narrow, winding streets.

So, Claire thought, she was not yet to meet the Treboul family? It looked as though her task would be as difficult as she had feared. Her task had seemed embarrassing from the beginning, but she had been hoping that the Trebouls would make some gesture which would ease her path.

Her gaze was abstracted as she stared out of the car window. She barely noticed the sights which, a few moments ago, had seemed so excitingly different.

Claire Stratton was the youngest daughter of a Cornish farmer, born and bred on the bleak, windswept acres of Trevillion, a square, stone farmhouse which looked out across turbulent seas from its green and rocky promontory.

The Stratton family had wrested a hard living from these windy fields for generations. Edward Stratton ran a few hardy sheep in the sheltered combe behind his house, grew potatoes and daffodils, and somehow managed to make a sufficient income.

It was not the life for someone who liked comfort or an easy time, but to Edward Stratton it was a satisfying existence. His only son, Paul, had automatically been sent to agricultural college, but during his last summer vacation had gone to the Loire valley to work in a vineyard, had met a French girl and married her. Madeleine Treboul's father had owned the large vineyard in which Paul had been working. After their marriage, Paul had settled down to run the business with his father-in-law and within three years had been in sole control while Monsieur Treboul retired to the coast of Provence.

Edward Stratton, wounded to the quick by his son's decision to stay in France, had refused to attend the wedding, and had not answered any of his son's letters.

Claire, anxious and unhappy, had kept up a correspondence with Paul, hoping to heal the breach at some time. Her mother had died shortly before Paul's marriage, and Claire had felt that it was this blow which had made her father so very bitter. Had their mother been alive, the situation might have been very different.

Even the birth of two grandchildren did not soften her father's anger. The fact that they were given French names seemed to make him angrier than ever, indeed.

"Jean-Paul!" he had snorted, pushing Paul's letter aside. "My grandson given a foreign name!"

"He'll be living in France, Dad," Claire had pointed out, gently. "It's quite natural!"

Edward Stratton had pulled on his boots and stamped off into the mist, banging the farmhouse door behind him. When he returned his manner was so

7

bleak that Claire dared not bring up the subject again.

She had longed to visit her brother and meet his wife, but her father had flown into a black rage at the very suggestion, and, fearing to precipitate a crisis in their relations, Claire had given way. She was deeply attached to her father, and felt a great compassion for his loneliness, although it was self-imposed. The passing of the years made no easier the loss of his only son. Edward Stratton turned inward, sombre and brooding, his pride growing like a cancer inside him. Love that is warped can soon turn to hate, and Claire often feared for her father's reason, seeing him torn between pride and a natural desire to see his son again.

After her mother's death, Claire had taken up the reins of the household, pushing aside her own dream of training as a nurse, and, although she was content enough, she sometimes felt that her life was too narrow and restricted. Trevillion was a lonely place. Their nearest neighbours were farmers, busy from dawn to dusk like themselves, and there was little social life.

The elder of the two Stratton daughters, Annette, had shaken the dust of Trevillion off her feet at an early age. She was now private secretary to a high-powered London tycoon, and lived in an elegant flat at the top of a tall Chelsea house looking out over the Thames. She rarely visited Trevillion, and when she did, looked at Claire with pitying derision.

"How do you stick the life here? Miles from anywhere! No shops, no fun! I'd go mad!"

Claire had gazed at her thoughtfully, shrugging slightly. Who else was there to look after Trevillion?

Who else would make sure that their father ate properly, changed his damp clothes on coming in and took sufficient rest? Claire sometimes suspected that left to himself, her father would become desperate from sheer loneliness and bitterness.

It was easy to give advice when one knew one would not be called upon to help in any way. Claire did not blame Annette for leaving the burden on her shoulders. Her beautiful red-headed sister was simply not cut out for a life of boredom and routine. The glamour and glitter of London were Annette's natural background, just as a warm valley in France best suited Paul. Now and then, though, it occurred to Claire that she had never yet had the chance to find out where she belonged. Fate had decreed that her duty should lie at Trevillion, and she accepted it without a struggle, since rebellion was useless. If she had any secret dreams, she kept them to herself.

Annette, a little guilty perhaps, tried to make amends by sending Claire parcels of pretty London clothes from time to time. Claire found it exciting to unwrap these bulky parcels, pulling out silky underwear, filmy tights, gay shirts and sweaters which looked out of place in the stone-flagged kitchen, but which brightened her few hours of leisure, and made her feel cheerful when she went shopping in the nearest market town on a Saturday morning.

Her life had seemed to be set in a quiet routine until the day, two months ago, when the telegram arrived.

Edward Stratton had taken it from the boy and opened it himself. Claire, busy in the larder, had heard a terrible groan, and ran into the kitchen in time to see her father slump to the floor, his face a shocking colour, his eyelids working violently.

Seeing the telegram on the floor, she had picked it up, read it and winced, the tears starting to her eyes, then hurried to her father with a look of anxious compassion.

The doctor, hastily summoned, had pronounced Edward Stratton to have had a stroke. "He'll recover in time, but he needs complete rest and good nursing."

They removed her father to hospital for a few weeks, during which time she haunted the waiting-rooms, and at last allowed him to return home to Trevillion where Claire could nurse him herself.

Claire had been too anxious and too busy to give more than a few snatched hours of thought to the news that the telegram had conveyed—the tragic deaths of Paul and his wife in a car accident. She had replied by telegram with the news of her father's stroke, and followed with a letter of condolence to the Treboul family, regretting that she would not be able to attend the funeral and asking for news of the two little children.

A stiff letter came back, thanking her for her kind words and assuring her that Jean-Paul and Marie-Claire were being well cared for and would lack nothing that love or money could provide. There was no reference to her father, but Claire had sighed, reading between the lines. Naturally the Treboul family would resent her father's attitude to their daughter. It was sad, though, that at this time of shared grief they could not all come together.

It was easy for her to understand and forgive her

father. Paul's desertion, so soon after his wife's death, had been a bitter blow to him. He had been like a lost soul for months. There had been an emptiness in the farmhouse, where once his wife had been the heart of the home, an absence as physically felt as pain. Claire, struggling to keep the home just as her mother had done, had felt it deeply. Her father, she knew, must feel it even more.

The Trebouls, who did not know him, could not realise how much he loved Paul, even while he was refusing to see him again. One had to know him to comprehend what made him do such cruel things.

As soon as her father began to respond to treatment, he began to fret over his unknown grandchildren. Paul's death had changed him. Now he wanted nothing in the world but to hold his grandson in his arms, and the doctor grew concerned at his condition, since his perpetual anxiety over the two children was a bar to his recovery.

Reluctant, nervous, Claire was persuaded to go to France to see the Trebouls. Annette's employer was in America for a month, and she surprisingly offered to come home to take charge at the farm while Claire was in France.

"Not even the prospect of a holiday in the South of France would persuade me to face a journey back to England with two weepy toddlers," she said frankly.

Their nearest neighbour, Peter Dillon, had been generous in his help since Edward Stratton fell ill, and his mother offered to come over and help Annette several times a week. Claire shrewdly suspected her of wishing to keep an eye on her son. Mrs. Dillon went in dread of Peter marrying. A widow for ten years, she doted on her only child, and kept him on a tight, if loving rein. A brief interlude, two years ago, when Peter and Claire had become very close, had been brought to an abrupt close when his mother found out, and Peter had avoided Claire since, with embarrassed, guilty eyes.

Claire wrote to the Trebouls, received a courteous but cool reply agreeing to her visit and confirming that she had been booked into a local hotel, then braced herself and set out for France. Her father, still pitifully weak, begged her to bring back the two children to England, and added that he was sure she would be able to persuade the Trebouls to agree to a long visit.

Feeling totally inadequate, she had travelled across France in comfortable trains, having decided not to fly since she wanted time in which to think. She suspected that her visit would be a disaster. She would not blame the Trebouls if they were hostile, but for her father's sake she was determined to try as hard as she could to win them over.

She was still engrossed in her own thoughts when the sleek grey car turned into a long drive, lined with palm trees, beyond which she could see smooth green lawns, neat and colourful flower beds full of roses, lavender, petunias and jasmine which scented the air, and brightly striped umbrellas fluttering above sun-loungers on which lay sunbathers in dark glasses and wide straw hats.

The chauffeur pulled up outside the long modern frontage, all shining plate glass and potted plants, and hurried round to assist her out of the back of the car, his capped head bent attentively towards her.

Claire looked up at the hotel with curiosity not un-mingled with amusement and a degree of panic. This place was a million years away from the stormy grandeur of Trevillion! She did not even dare to guess how much it would cost her to stay here for so much as one night. Why had the Trebouls booked her in here?

The chauffeur was waiting, her one shabby case in his hand, and she hurriedly followed him into the hotel. A uniformed hall porter watched them advance, his expression loftily incredulous, but a very smart young man moved forward from the polished teak desk, bowing and greeting her by name. Clearly, she decided, she had been brought to the right place.

"Will you sign the register, Mademoiselle Stratton?" His smooth olive-skinned face was bent forward to watch her sign, then he handed the nearest page-boy a key-ring and bowed to Claire once more. "We have put you in the Regency Suite, *mademoiselle*."

Claire was too startled to respond. Nervelessly she followed the page-boy towards the lifts at the rear of the reception hall, walking warily over deep carpeted floors, past comfortable leather chairs, none of which was in use at present.

A suite! She repeated the words with disbelief. The Trebouls must be out of their minds! She had expected them to book her into some quiet pension somewhere, somewhere pleasantly inexpensive, not this glittering palace of the idle rich!

She was so absorbed that she did not notice where

13

she was going, and bumped into a couple emerging from some inner sanctum of this palatial establishment, sending a bag carried by one of them spinning across the hall.

Flushing, she murmured an apology for her clumsiness. These people were typical of the normal guests at the hotel, she saw. Their clothes stamped them. Elegant, expensive, carried like the banner of an army, they wore clothes with cool hauteur and calm self-assurance.

The woman into whom she had bumped was at least in her late twenties, yet looked younger at a first glance, very French, with smooth black hair worn swathed on top of her fine-boned head, discreetly made-up black eyes with thick lashes, and a full, scarlet mouth. Claire gazed at her with envy. That light-weight suit in champagne silk, the rose-tinted pearls clasped round her throat, the perfume which drifted around her, subtle and heady as wine! She was a luxury item, Claire decided, and she knew it.

Her sophistication made Claire feel even more out of place, burningly conscious of the cheapness of her own home-made sailor suit, which had seemed so smart in Cornwall, with its crisp white collar and full navy-blue skirt.

The man, who had moved away to retrieve the bag, now returned and glanced at Claire smilingly, handing the cream object to its owner. He was the perfect partner, Claire decided, for that very chic Frenchwoman. Tall, olive-skinned and black-haired, his eyes were surprisingly grey under thin dark brows, his suit very formal in this climate. The fleshless cheeks and jutting jaw gave an impression of arrogance and power, underlined by the thin, firm mouth.

Something inside her tightened, she grew stiff and hostile, her eyes hurriedly withdrawn from their too open scrutiny of his insufferably handsome face. How dared he look at her with that slight mockery, that faint lift of the eyebrows, as though she were a visitor from outer space?

The lift was waiting, the page-boy carefully blank as he held the doors open. The dark man stepped aside, waving a well-shaped hand for Claire to step past into the lift. She did so, head held high, avoiding his eyes. One glance from that amused and probing grey gaze was enough!

Within seconds the doors had closed and the lift was in motion, smoothly purring upwards. She sighed, relaxing. It was going to be an ordeal, staying here, surrounded by people like that. As soon as possible she would have to find a more suitable hotel, somewhere small and quiet, where she would not be exposed to the patronising amusement of the wealthy. Those two had made her feel like a housemaid coming to the front door by mistake!

The page-boy conducted her to a white door, numbered in gilt, which he flung open with a grand gesture. The first appalled glance made Claire want to turn round and run out of the hotel. She got a first impression of deep-piled carpets, high, gleaming windows and elegant, honey-coloured teak furniture. Brocade-covered armchairs faced each other across a low coffee table, shelves held delicate glass ornaments and glazed porcelain, a writing table stood between the windows, bearing a low bowl of beautifully arranged flowers.

The boy was carrying her case into the bedroom, and she dumbly followed. The bed was draped with a fitted silk spread in palest pink; the carpet was a shade deeper and the dressing-table was ornate French Empire, finely balanced on slim legs and gilded with curling bows and clusters of flowers. Through the open bathroom door she could see that even the towels were deep-piled and deliciously soft, their lemon shade just slightly paler than the colour of the bath.

Indicating the telephone beside the bed, the boy said, "If you need anything at any hour, please to call the desk. I hope you will enjoy your stay here, *mademoiselle*."

She nervously fumbled at her handbag, but, reading her mind, he smiled and moved away. "No tips, please. . . ." His tone was polite, yet she flushed, feeling even more clumsy and shy. To her relief he then softly departed, and she was alone.

She wandered about the suite, examining everything with admiration and alarm. Then she took out her travellers cheques and counted them uneasily. Just one night in this suite was certainly going to make quite a big hole in her money. Of course, she could wire Annette to send her some more, but she did not want to do that while her father was still so weak. She would have to be even more careful with her money, that was all. It was a pity, but she would manage somehow.

It amused her to compare this place with her own old-fashioned bedroom at Trevillion, with its heavy

16

oak furniture, chintz curtains and patchwork quilt, made by her grandmother in the long, dark evenings of the years between the two world wars. Her grandmother would have stared in half-shocked amazement to see her here!

She paused before the dressing-table and studied her own reflection. Slender, of medium height, she had the fresh complexion of someone who has been accustomed to years of open-air life, and she had never seen any need to embellish it with much in the way of cosmetics. But now her pink lipstick and thinly applied powder seemed childishly unsophisticated, compared with the make-up so artistically used by the woman she had seen downstairs. She gazed at herself, pushing back her straight lint-white hair, grimacing with self-disgust.

Annette was right! She did need to take herself in hand. It had never mattered at Trevillion, but she saw things in quite a new light here in St. Hilaire. She must buy some new make-up, experiment a little.

Her dark blue eyes examined her face with some depression. There seemed little one could do about a small, tip-tilted nose, over-thin cheeks and very ordinary eyes. She did not see the purity and delicacy of her oval face, or notice the width and brilliance of her eyes set beneath their silky pale fringe of hair. Searching for more obvious beauty, she failed to appreciate the things which made her different; the fine bone structure, the gentleness of her mouth, above all her lovely eyes.

She was just wondering how she could get in touch with the Trebouls when a tap on the door made her jump. Swallowing, she invited the new arrival to enter.

Her visitor was a middle-aged Frenchman, dapper, dark and charming. His dark eyes flattered her discreetly as he bowed.

"Mademoiselle Stratton? I am the hotel manager, Pierre Frautbois. Monsieur de Carceron asked me to make certain you had everything you require. If there is anything I can do for you, please mention it. Is your suite comfortable?"

"Oh, very comfortable," stammered Claire, feeling totally in the dark. Why was she getting this millionaire treatment? Was it possible that the Trebouls had some mistaken notion of her father's wealth?

The manager bowed again. "That is excellent. Monsieur de Carceron begged you to do him the honour of dining with him tonight at eight o'clock."

Baffled, Claire asked, "Monsieur de Carceron? I'm afraid I don't know. . . ."

"The owner of this hotel, *mademoiselle*," the other man explained. "He is a friend of Monsieur Treboul, you understand."

"Oh!" That did explain something, Claire supposed, but she was not quite sure what.

"Will Monsieur Treboul be dining too?" Surely, she thought, the Trebouls would make an appearance soon?

The manager looked politely blank. "Perhaps," he said vaguely. "May I assure Monsieur de Carceron that you will dine with him, *mademoiselle*?"

She agreed doubtfully, and he left, smiling his admiration. Drifting into the bathroom, she took a leisurely shower and, smelling deliciously of the scented bath salts provided by the hotel, dressed with care and some misgivings for her dinner engagement.

Her one evening dress, reluctantly packed at Annette's half scornful insistence, was simplicity itself. A straight sheath in midnight blue nylon, with floating filmy sleeves which fell to her wrists, she had made it herself and only worn it once.

She wondered what Monsieur de Carceron was like as she made her way down to reception once more. Middle-aged, like the hotel manager, presumably, if he was a friend of Monsieur Treboul. Slightly plump, she decided, with a balding head and gallant, kindly, paternal manners. She hoped he would be easy to talk to, since she must soon break it to him that she could not afford to stay in his luxury hotel.

When she walked across to the reception desk, the clerk smiled attentively. She gave her name, and he picked up the telephone and spoke softly into it in rapid French.

"Monsieur will be here directly," he told her, replacing the receiver.

She nodded and turned to find a seat, only to halt in dismay and disbelief as she saw the man approaching her.

"Good evening, Miss Stratton," he said blandly. "We meet again." The thin eyebrows arched mockingly at the expression in her wide eyes.

Pulling herself together, she forced a smile, but inwardly she protested against fate. Why did it have to be this man? Surely there must be some mistake, yet she knew, with a sinking feeling, that there was none.

"Monsieur de Carceron?" she questioned in a tone which somehow came out stiff and hostile.

He inclined his head with the same irritating amusement.

Claire could not suppress the sigh of dismay which escaped. The thought of spending several hours in his company was quite unbearable. All her confidence, her shreds of self-respect, seemed to be seeping away rapidly already.

"I think," he said coolly, studying her, "we should go straight in to dinner."

His hand beneath her elbow, he steered her through the discreetly separated tables towards one which was partially screened from the rest of the diners by a trellis supporting ivy and a plant starred with small pink flowers which she could not identify.

A further pang of apprehension gripped her as the waiter presented her with a leather-bound menu. Yet another hurdle for her to face! She might have enjoyed finding her way through the unfamiliar French names in any other company, but in his she felt miserably inadequate. She studied it wildly, all her French seeming to have deserted her, and found nothing familiar.

"Will you permit me?" The soft, mocking voice made her jump.

His shrewd grey eyes were watching her, his hand outstretched to take the menu from her limp fingers.

Hands folded in her lap to stop them trembling, she listened as he swiftly ordered. The waiter bowed and departed on silent feet. He leaned back and studied her with calm interest.

"So! You are Paul's little sister?"

"You knew my brother?"

He shrugged the broad shoulders whose strength was only partly disguised by elegant dark cloth. "But very well. It was tragic, that accident. I was deeply shocked to hear the news."

"It almost killed my father when he heard," she said soberly, nodding.

His eyes narrowed. "Your father showed no concern for Paul while he was alive!"

Claire sat upright, chin lifting defiantly, but before she could retort, he had spoken again.

"I am sorry if that offends you. I had no right to comment, but Paul had so often talked of this to me, and I cannot help remembering how hurt he was by your father's narrow-minded insularity."

Claire knew how true that was, yet she was angry to hear this stranger talking about her father with such harshness.

"My father was hurt, too," she retorted. "Strattons have farmed Trevillion for two centuries. My father had the right to expect that his son would carry on the tradition, particularly as Paul seemed to love farming. Now the farm will have to be sold, unless. . . ." She broke off, flushing, thinking that all this was too private to be discussed with him.

He leaned forward, his gaze acute. "Unless you marry someone who is prepared to take on the burden of farming barren acres?" he questioned.

"Trevillion is not barren! We farm intensively, and make a reasonable profit. My father is deeply proud of our home."

"And you?" he asked.

"I?" For a moment she was confused.

"Are you proud of this bleak farm in the remote tip of Cornwall? I seem to remember your brother speculating on whether you would marry a local farmer, and carry on at Trevillion when your father retired."

"I love my home, naturally," she said coolly.

"And the young man . . . what was his name? Peter something? Is he happy to take on the double task of farming Trevillion as well as his own farm? Or do you also demand sacrifices from those you love? Would you want him to devote himself to Trevillion alone?"

Claire was both surprised and angry. She remembered mentioning Peter Dillon from time to time in her letters to Paul, but she had not imagined that Paul would read so much into her brief and rather vague references. Why he should have discussed it with this man she could not conceive! And how dared he now quiz her about Peter as though he had the right to ask such personal questions!

Her voice was chilly and formal as she replied. "I really don't see why you should ask me such questions, *monsieur.*"

He shrugged, his lean features suddenly reserved. "I apologise! I have been so accustomed to hearing about you from Paul that I forgot that to you we are strangers. Paul used to read parts of your letters to me."

"Really?" Her voice somehow conveyed both incredulity and a withdrawn coldness. She felt distinctly at a disadvantage, since he knew so much about her, and she knew so little of him. Paul had, she remembered now, often mentioned a close friend whom he simply referred to as Louis. This must be the man, she supposed. She could remember very little of what Paul had said, but she had gained an impression that he lived in the Loire valley, not here on the coast of Provence.

The waiter began to serve the meal, which Claire was relieved to find quite simple. Hors d'oeuvres; a concoction of cod stuffed with prawn, then veal smothered in a smooth sauce, followed by a sorbet.

They ate in an uneasy silence. From time to time her companion made some polite remark and she answered briefly.

They withdrew to his private office for coffee. It was a large, masculine room, starkly furnished with a brown leather-topped desk, brown leather chairs and a metal filing cabinet. The windows were covered with white blinds and it gave a general impression of efficiency and austerity. She found it surprising after the luxury of the hotel.

He helped her to a chair, indicated a box of cigarettes and when she shook her head helped himself to one and lit it.

The waiter tapped and entered with the coffee. He was dismissed immediately with a nod.

"Black or white?"

Claire murmured that she would prefer white, and he poured her coffee, placed the cup before her, poured himself a cup and sat down behind his desk with it.

Now, she thought, he'll tell me when I'm to meet the Trebouls, and how soon I will see little Jean-Paul and Marie-Claire. She looked at him with hopeful, parted lips and eager eyes.

"Mademoiselle," he began crisply, "Monsieur Treboul has asked me to speak with you. I know your reason for being here, and he wishes you to understand clearly that it is out of the question for the children to go to England."

CHAPTER TWO

CLAIRE was dumb for a moment, her gaze incredulous. She was refused permission to take the two children to England before she had even met them! A slow anger began to burn inside her as she remembered her father's desperate, deep-sunken eyes. The hope of seeing his two grandchildren was all that he had to cling to now that Paul was dead. The Trebouls had no right to deny it to him.

Louis de Carceron waited for her to speak, his brown hands lying on the desk, palm down, the long, strong fingers immobile.

"They can't expect me to accept such an arbitrary decision before they've even seen me!" Her voice was tightly controlled, but she had to press her nails into her palms to stop herself from losing her temper altogether. "And why you? Why should this concern an outsider? It seems very odd for them to ask you to intervene in such a delicate, personal matter."

"I am not exactly an outsider," he said flatly. "I am Jean-Paul's godfather. He is named for me—my first name is Jean, but I am called Louis." He inclined his narrow head towards her. "It would please me if you used my name, Claire." The soft inflection of his voice as he said her own name brought a small coin of bright carnation into each cheek, but she pressed her lips together firmly, still very angry.

"I still don't see why you should be involved! This concerns only the two families."

"In France, the godfather is more than a mere symbol," he said calmly. "We take the duties of the godparent very seriously. I feel it my duty, since Paul's death, to regard myself as being responsible for Jean-Paul, in both material and spiritual matters."

She stared at him. "Jean-Paul has relatives who are more than happy to be responsible for him!"

"It seems to me that some of them think only of the child as an object for possession. They do not consider his true welfare, but only their own desires." His voice was incisive and his grey eyes cold as a winter sea.

She flushed. "You refer to my father, I presume?"

He shrugged without answering.

"You're wrong!" Her voice was a little shaky. "He's not asking for control over Jean-Paul. He only asks to see him from time to time. A short holiday in England can do the children no harm, after all! Surely my father has the right to see his own grandchildren?"

"They are too young for such a journey," he returned. "You must consider what it would do to them to be removed from familiar and comforting surroundings so soon after the loss of their parents."

She was very still, her dark blue eyes wide. "They know that Paul and Madeleine are dead?" Her voice was hushed and incredulous.

He lifted one thin eyebrow. "They naturally asked questions. It is wrong to lie in such a case. They were told very gently."

She trembled, clasping her hands together. "Marie-Claire is only two years old!"

"She understood, nevertheless, that her parents had gone to live with Jesus," he said gently. "At that age it is easy to accept such things. It is only later that the mind questions such simple truths."

"It was cruel! A baby . . . poor little baby!" Claire's eyes were wet with unshed tears and she looked at him with loathing.

"You are too emotional," he pronounced sharply. "When one is dealing with small children it is a mistake to be over-emotional. One must be calm and certain at all times, or one disturbs them. It is as well that the Trebouls have sent them away."

She sat up, stiffening. "What do you mean?"

He spread his hands on the desk. "When they learnt of your impending arrival, they decided to send the children to stay with relatives who have children of a similar age. It seemed best that the children should have no suspicion of any argument over them. When you have come to terms with the Trebouls, they will be brought back home."

"Just like that!" She was furious now, her cheeks quite white with rage. "I never heard of anything so . . ."

"Control yourself!" He rose and came round the desk, leaning over her with cold grey eyes searching her face. "Madame Treboul was deeply grieved by the loss of her only child. She adores her grandchildren and would go to any lengths to protect them."

"I can understand that, of course," Claire admitted, sighing. "But I have to consider my own father. He has been so ill. He may not live long. Surely it's understandable that he should wish to see the children? If he could travel, he would be here himself."

His thin mouth was twisted cynically. "Even though he has ignored their existence until now? Though he refused to come to Paul's wedding? Has not answered one of his letters?" His tone was icily contemptuous. "Do you expect the Trebouls to believe that such a man is to be trusted? Do you expect them to trust their precious grandchildren to such a heartless man?"

"My father loved Paul! He may have been stubborn, even cruel, but you must test his behaviour by the hurt Paul inflicted on him!"

"By marrying a French girl?" His face took on an angry, alien cast as he snapped out the question.

"By refusing to come home to Trevillion," Claire said hotly. "By turning his back on all that my father has lived for, all that he believes in!"

There was a long silence. Then he straightened, shrugging. "Mademoiselle, I have performed my task. Madame Treboul will not permit you to see the children until you have accepted that they cannot go to England."

"How can she refuse me permission to see my own brother's children? I don't believe it's legally possible!"

"She is their legal guardian," he told her flatly. "Paul named her in his will and gave her full charge of the children."

Claire rose, her eyes distressed. "I can't believe he intended her to refuse me access to the children!"

He looked away, frowning. "Paul, alas, is no longer with us. Madame has charge of the children, and her decision is final. If you will promise not to talk to the children about their grandfather, or try to take them to England, you may visit them." He looked back at her. "They are not in St. Hilaire, so do not imagine you will be able to visit them without her permission."

"It's . . . it's monstrous!"

He caught hold of her elbow, his thin fingers biting into her. "Let me advise you to be sensible! Do not lose your temper. Think the matter over. If you can make friends with Madame Treboul your battle will be half won. She will only be antagonised by emotional scenes."

Claire shook his hand from her arm. "I neither need nor desire your advice, *monsieur*. Goodnight."

When she was safely back in her suite, she sat down to consider the situation, with hopeless anger. It had never occurred to her that the Trebouls would be this difficult! She had anticipated a little stiffness, even hostility, but such cold, determined opposition was alarming.

Her thoughts went round in ever-decreasing circles, without arriving at any conclusion, and in the end she went to bed without having reached a decision.

Surprisingly, she slept well and awoke to a bright morning and the sound of china clinking. A smiling French maid was standing at the bedside, a cup of tea in her hand.

"*Bonjour!*" Claire sat up, eager to test out her French, and the maid's smile broadened.

"Good morning, *mademoiselle*," she replied in the same language. "I have laid out your breakfast in the

29

salon, by the window. I thought you might like some tea in bed before you got up."

"That was very kind of you," Claire said, accepting the cup with a sigh of delight. "What's your name?"

"Marie." The girl curtsied, smiling still. "Is there anything else?"

Claire shook her head and Marie departed. During the years since Paul's marriage, Claire had taught herself French from books and a set of gramophone records, and had longed for the chance to practise. It was, she decided, a great pity that the French were so fluent in English as it made it harder for her to try out her French.

When she learnt French she had hoped to please Paul's wife by being able to talk to her in her own language. Now she would never have the opportunity.

She sighed, finished her tea and got up. After a quick shower, she dressed in a white cotton sweater and blue jeans, ate some of the fruit and croissants left by the maid, drank some coffee, and went down to reception. The hall was deserted, except for a desk clerk who regarded her without much curiosity.

Claire went out into the gardens, following a flower-edged path which, she found, led to the back of the hotel. Here she found an open-air swimming pool, with unbelievably blue water in which some guests were already swimming lazily. It was flanked by sun-bathing areas, gay with umbrellas and little white iron-work tables, sun-loungers and tubs of flowers.

A waiter in a white coat was serving coffee to some men in very brief trunks, who turned to glance at

Claire with the admiring interest of all Frenchmen when they see an attractive young woman.

She wandered on, gazing around with curiosity, and found herself at the top of a flight of steps which led to the beach. The air was sweet as wine, the freshness of morning lingering like the scent of flowers. Blue sky, blue sea, golden sand . . . it was all so much like the photographs in a travel brochure! Not quite real, yet temptingly beautiful.

She looked along the curving outline of the coast and saw villas and hotels, shimmering through the last remnants of the early morning heat haze, as insubstantial and lovely as dream palaces built on clouds.

Strolling along the beach, avoiding a few early sun-worshippers, she took another path which led up towards the centre of the town. On her left stretched the old part of the town, the fishing village, rambling, picturesque and untidy. Soon she was walking through an open-air market, already crowded and noisy, the stalls vivid with flowers and fruit, piled with vegetables, eggs and fish.

Claire lingered here, watching dark-clad women with weathered faces buying with the shrewdness and caution of good housewives, listening to the French which rattled like machine-gun fire on all sides. She found it difficult to understand half of it because of the speed and clipped accents, but she gradually distinguished the cries of those trying to persuade customers to buy.

She paused at one stall to buy a straw basket, deep and capacious, with red and green flowers sewn along the sides. It delighted her to test her French, and to see the pleased grin with which the stallholder greeted her attempt to speak his language. Shyly she counted out her money, and he nodded approval, appraising her silky pale hair and delicate features with the dark eye of an expert.

She walked out of the market and found a street café, quiet at this hour, and sat down under one of the red-striped umbrellas. A young waiter came out and bent over her, his slanting black eyes flirtatious. "Yes, *mademoiselle*?"

She ordered coffee and he brought it at once, fragrant and steaming, in a blue enamel pot. It was exhilarating to sit there in the sunshine, sipping her coffee and watching the people pass. Old men in berets, riding bicycles; pretty girls with golden skins and sleek hair; old women with white scarves over their heads and heavy baskets in their hands.

Claire heard the melodic chime of the church clock, and saw that it was time she made her way back to the hotel. She still had to find an inexpensive hotel, but she felt too happy to do anything about it at the moment. She would think of it after lunch.

In the reception hall she met Pierre Frautbois. "You have been into the town?" he asked, eyeing her basket.

She told him eagerly about her little exploration, and he smiled, especially when she boasted of her essay into French.

"So! You speak our language?"

Blushing, she replied in French, "I hope to improve my accent while I'm here, but I find French people so kind and so good at English that it's hard to get the practice !"

He laughed. "You need not worry, *mademoiselle*. You have a very pretty accent already. Your English accent makes our language sound quite charming, I assure you." Then he glanced at his watch. "Will you do me the honour of taking lunch? I should like to talk to you, and it may help your French !"

She accepted cheerfully, went up to her suite and changed into her sailor suit, surveying her scanty wardrobe with dismay. She really must find a cheaper hotel ! Her clothes just did not fit these luxurious surroundings.

When she rejoined Pierre they went into the dining-room at once. He seated her, proffered the menu and was happy to wait patiently while she carefully deciphered it, choosing melon to begin with, a seafood salad to follow, and fresh fruit instead of the tempting desserts which she suspected would add inches to her waistline. At Trevillion she ate freely, because she was so busy that it made no difference to her weight, but she was leading an idle life here and must adapt her diet accordingly.

When the waiter had served them with slices of ice-cold melon, dusted with ginger, Pierre smiled and said, "Before we begin, I wish to dispose of one embarrassing subject." He gave one of those eloquent Gallic gestures which make a conversation in France so interesting, a broad shrug combined with a wave of the hand, almost supplying a whole dictionary of comment upon a topic without using a single word. "Louis asked me to mention that your suite is provided free of charge, since you are the sister of his very dear Paul."

Claire's fingers tightened on her fork. "Free of charge?" She felt her cheeks beginning to glow hotly.

Pierre shrugged again, avoiding her gaze. "It is a difficult matter for him to broach, of course. He did not wish you to be embarrassed."

"It's very kind of him," Claire said stiffly, "but please tell him I insist upon paying for my suite!"

Anxiously, Pierre said, "Louis never charges when one of his friends or relatives comes to stay here, I assure you!"

"I'm neither," she said sharply. "We're total strangers, and I must insist on paying." She would not be under any such obligation to that man. "I shall, in any case, be leaving today."

Pierre was aghast. "Leaving? You are not happy in our hotel? Someone has offended you? The service is not good? Please tell me what makes you unhappy, and I shall see to it that it is put right immediately."

"Everyone has been most kind," she said unhappily, Then, staring down at her melon with unseeing eyes, "I . . . I can't afford to stay here, that's all. I expected to stay in a quiet pension . . . I shall find one this afternoon, and move there at once."

He sighed, eyeing her with comprehension. "You are offended that Louis offers you your suite without payment, yes?"

Her dark blue eyes blazed. "Yes! Frankly, I am. I prefer to pay my own way."

He looked thoughtful. "I wish you could meet my son Léon. I would like him to know a girl like you.

You would be good for him, I think. He takes life too easily, he has no sense of responsibility. Money, to Léon, is easily acquired, quickly spent. He has never known what it is to be in need."

"How old is he?" Claire looked at him with interest. He had a melancholy look, and she could sense his deep sadness about his son.

"Twenty-four," he shrugged. "Yet he behaves still like an adolescent. Louis is weary of his escapades. He has persuaded me to cut off his allowance, to make him work. Léon has gone to Le Petit Trésor to learn all about the making of wine."

"Le Petit Trésor?" she asked idly.

"Louis's small chateau. You have not heard of it? Ah, it is a gem. It was built by his family under the Sun King, as a country house, which is how it acquired its name. The Little Treasure, they called it, when it was finished. It was intended as a model estate, you understand. For many years now it has made wine of the finest. Golden as the sun, clear as morning dew, with a bouquet to make one drunk! Louis spends six months of the year there, from the wine harvest to the late spring."

"Nice for him," Claire commented drily. She remembered now where she had heard of Louis before. Paul had often written about Le Petit Trésor, but somehow she had not made the connection when she came here and met Louis.

Pierre looked quickly at her, raising his eyebrows. "You are an unusual girl, *mademoiselle*!"

"Please, call me Claire," she urged. "And why am I so unusual?"

His liquid dark eyes beamed at her. "Ah, Claire . . . what a pretty name, and it suits you, with your hair like still moonlight, and your midnight blue eyes!"

She laughed. "Only a Frenchman could·turn so charming a compliment. Now an Englishman would say. . . ." She looked impish and dropped her voice to a gruff whisper. "You're a decent sort, Claire!"

He threw up his square hands, lamenting, "The English have no eyes!"

"You still haven't told me why I'm unusual," she reminded him, laughing.

He gave her a quick, shrewd glance. "You seem impervious to the dangerous charms of my friend Louis, Claire—that is what I meant. He has only to smile at most women to have them swooning like adolescents at his feet. It will be good for him, I think, to be taught that he is not all-conquering."

She blushed and looked away. "Oh." There was a little pause, then she asked if he could recommend a good pension, and he evasively promised to see what he could find out for her.

"I hope you will be here for the carnival next week. It is very gay and colourful. I am hoping that Louis will permit my son to visit me while it is on, and I would like to introduce him to you."

He was a little too obvious, she decided, as she went up to her suite to take a short rest during the afternoon. Clearly, Pierre was eager to find some sensible girl to take care of his son, and she just suited the bill. She wondered if the French still arranged marriages for their children. She did not think they did, but Pierre's dream of an anchor for his wandering boy was definitely along those lines. It would be funny if it were not so pathetic. Poor Pierre! Like her own father, he could not resist trying to run his son's life for him.

She was lying down on her bed, with the blinds lowered and the room masked in blue shadow, when the telephone rang.

"I would like to speak to you at once," said an unmistakable voice in crisp tones.

Claire felt her pulses leap queerly, and her irritation made her snap a little. "I'm taking a siesta, on the advice of your hotel manager."

There was a pause. "The matter is urgent," he said flatly.

She sighed. "Very well, I'll come down."

"No need," he said quickly. "I will come to your suite."

Claire put down the receiver and slipped off the bed. Her hair was tousled, her cheeks flushed and her eyes still drowsy with sleep. She brushed her hair, applied lipstick and powder and went into the sitting-room in time to open the door to his sharp tap.

She saw at once that he was angry. The grey eyes were narrowed and brilliant, the firm mouth tight, the head held at a belligerent angle.

"So!" He walked past her, smiling coldly, and looked around the room. "You are leaving us, I hear!"

"Yes," she said hurriedly. "I'm not accustomed to places like this and I would prefer somewhere quieter."

"That is very interesting," he snapped. "It is also quite out of the question."

"I'll make my own decisions," she said indignantly.

37

"You are a young woman in a foreign country. Monsieur Treboul placed you under my roof because he wished to make certain you were quite safe. I will not permit you to leave it while you are in France."

"You will not permit?" She was breathless with anger by now, her own eyes wide with disbelief. "What right have you . . ."

"I will not argue with you!" He turned aside loftily, shrugging. "I stand in lieu of a brother to you. You will stay!"

"I shall certainly do nothing of the kind! I'm over twenty-one, and even my own father would never dare to speak to me in such an overbearing fashion!"

"English girls have too much freedom," he dismissed arrogantly. "While you are in France you will behave differently. In this hotel you are easily protected. If you went elsewhere it would be impossible to make sure that you were always safe."

"I prefer to be independent," Claire protested. "I don't wish to be under any obligation to you!"

He drew in his lip, his eyes narrowing further. "What are you saying?" In his anger his accent became more obviously French. "That I may use my hospitality in some underhand way? Demand a *quid pro quo*?" The thin dark brows rose derisively, and suddenly the grey eyes sparkled with mockery. "I assure you, Claire, you do not need to fear that I shall try to persuade you to pay for your suite by surrendering to my amorous attentions."

Her cheeks and throat were dipped in scarlet. "I didn't imagine you would!"

"No?" His voice was silky as he looked down at

her, eyes taunting. She involuntarily stepped back and was furious to hear him laugh softly. "You are easily alarmed, Claire."

Then his mood changed abruptly. He turned away and walked to the window, gazing out in silence with his back to her.

After a moment he turned back and smiled with sudden and insufferable charm. "Come, Claire," his voice lingering on her name in a way that made her angrily conscious of him. "There is no need for us to be opposed to each other. I was Paul's friend. I wish to be yours."

"You were Paul's friend," she said flatly. "But now you are Monsieur Treboul's friend."

"And that means we must be enemies? Surely not!"

"It means you support him against my father."

"You are very attached to this stubborn father of yours," he said slowly. "And, I begin to think, very like him."

She laughed, suddenly amused by the idea. "I don't look like my father at all. Paul was more like him than I am."

"Not physically, perhaps, but in your attitudes. You, too, are stubborn. You have a way of lifting your head in defiance, a way of looking obstinately determined. It is odd in so feminine a creature!"

She looked down, plaiting her fingers behind her back. She would not allow herself to be swayed by the warmth of his charm, or that insidiously teasing smile of his. For her father's sake, she must remain aloof from those who stood between him and the two children. All her loyalty lay at Trevillion.

He watched her bent head for a moment, his eyes intent, then said reasonably, "I have a suggestion to make. The Trebouls dine with me tonight." She looked up eagerly. "I suggest you dine with us. We will meet as friends, in a sociable atmosphere. There will be no mention of this dispute between you. You will get to know one another calmly and quietly, as though everything were normal. That way you may begin to comprehend each other's motives without misunderstanding or suspicion." He lifted one eyebrow, smiling down into her eyes. "Will you agree to that?"

Claire hesitated, then nodded, seeing the logic of his argument. It would make it easier if she met the Trebouls for the first time in an easy atmosphere, with a fourth person present, making it less of an ordeal and more of a social occasion.

He smiled, relaxing. "Good! And you will say no more about leaving the hotel? If you feel constrained by being here as my private guest, tell yourself that I do it for your brother. The Trebouls would probably have invited you to stay with them, had the circumstances been different. We do not like to break the laws of hospitality. I suggested you stay here as a . . . how do you say . . . compromise measure?"

She found herself smiling back. "You're very kind. I will stay. Thank you."

His gaze was gently teasing. "That was hard for you to say, no? Your pride had to be swallowed! Well, good! Pride is a hard taskmaster." He walked to the door. "Until tonight, then, Claire. . . ."

She stared at the closed door. He accused her of being proud! She had never met anyone so clearly ruled by pride as Louis de Carceron. It cloaked him from head to foot, pride of race, pride of birth, pride of manhood.

When the heat of the day subsided a little and a gentle breeze crept in from the sea, she sauntered down into town again, to buy some postcards and post her first letter to her father.

She had thought carefully about how much she should tell him of the situation. It would do no good to worry him at this stage. She wrote only that she was to meet the Trebouls that evening, and that the two children were at present staying with relatives, but would be home soon. She hoped to see them then, she added vaguely. She described the hotel in some detail, stressing the kindness of the Trebouls in arranging for her to stay there, but for some reason could not bring herself to mention the arrogant but charming owner.

When she had posted her letter, bought and written some cards for Annette, Peter and other local friends, she found her way back to the same quiet little café at which she had taken coffee.

The same waiter rushed to bring her a pot of tea and some delicious little cakes. While she was sipping her tea and nibbling one of the cakes, an English voice spoke at her elbow.

"Would you think me fresh if I asked if I might join you? I'm longing to hear an English voice again."

Startled, she looked up, and saw a man in his late twenties, lean and fair and very obviously English, with knowledgeable blue eyes, a charmingly rakish smile and a general air of pleasant cynicism. His blue shirt lay open at the throat, his blue jeans were clean but well worn, his skin a weathered bronze.

"How do you know I'm English?" she asked in French, curious, amused, yet suspecting that he was not a very desirable acquaintance.

He flipped her an engaging grin. "You've got to be joking. With hair like that, you have to be either Swedish or English, and one doesn't see Swedish girls dressed with that particular brand of English-rose simplicity. Nor do they dreamily sip a cup of tea as though it were nectar. Made in England is stamped all over you."

Claire laughed, not sure that she found his comments very flattering.

The waiter came out, and her new friend ordered a pot of tea for himself. Then he leaned back, lighting a cigarette, gazing at Claire with interest.

"Where are you staying? The Pension Albert? Or. . . ."

She broke in, smiling, "The Hotel St. Hilaire."

He sat up, choking on his smoke. When he had coughed into silence, he said, "I must be losing my touch. I would have put you in quite a different income bracket."

She grinned, "I am!" His chagrin at having made such a mistake amused her. "I'm staying there as a personal guest of the owner."

"You are a friend of Louis's?" He looked distinctly alarmed. "Glory! He'd skin me if he found out I'd picked you up in a café!" He ran a hand through his sun-blanched hair. "You won't tell him, will you? He would have me run out of town."

Claire laughed, "Don't be silly!"

To her amazement, he gazed at her soberly. "I'm not kidding, I assure you. You obviously don't know Louis very well. He is very much Lord High Executioner around here. And he has strict ideas of what he permits in this little town. I am one of the doubtful characters he would like to see the back of—and my picking you up would give him the excuse he needs."

CHAPTER THREE

CLAIRE stared in stupefied amazement for a moment, absorbing this information. It fitted with what she had seen of Louis de Carceron's character, certainly, yet it seemed incredibly out of date that one man should have such power to dominate a small community.

She said as much, and her companion gave a soft hoot of amusement. "I would give anything to see Louis's face if he could hear you! I bet no one has ever said that to him! He's used to a general air of reverence from the people around here."

She nodded. "I had noticed a waft of incense whenever he entered a room!"

He laughed again, eyeing her with interest. "Your looks are deceptive, aren't they? You can get quite a sting into your voice. Shall be introduce ourselves? I'm Tony Kirk." He held out his hand and she smilingly accepted it.

"I'm Claire Stratton."

He snapped his fingers. "I should have realised! So you're Paul Stratton's sister? I met your brother once or twice. I was sorry to hear about the accident. He was a good sort."

She smiled her thanks. "What do you do for a living, Mr. Kirk? Are you here on holiday?"

He shook his head. "I live here. I'm a writer,

mainly on travel. I turn in a few freelance articles whenever I run out of cash, which is pretty often, but I really want to write books."

"Novels?" she asked, rather impressed.

"No, travel books," he said lightly. "I've always wanted to explore foreign parts. When I was a boy I used to read nothing but travel books, and as soon as I could I started to travel. I ended up here by accident. I was on my way to Marseilles to take a boat to Africa when I met an old friend who had a house in the fishing village here. He wanted to go back home, so I took on the lease for a year. And here I've been ever since."

"It's a pleasant place to be, I suppose," she said politely.

He shrugged. "I'd move on if. . . ." he halted, glancing at her oddly.

Claire looked up at the church clock and saw that it was time she went back to the hotel. Tony rose with her, insisted on paying the bill and walked along beside her.

"Look, Claire . . . you don't mind if I call you Claire, do you?"

She smiled, shaking her head.

"Good. Claire, I think you might be able to help me. Would you be prepared to do me a favour? It will cost you nothing but a little time, I promise you."

She hesitated. "I can't promise until I hear what it is," she pointed out.

"Fair enough," he nodded. "It's a little involved, though, and I can't explain properly in a few minutes. Will you meet me tonight?"

"I'm sorry," she said, "I'm dining with someone else."

"Oh!" He looked discouraged and she felt sorry for him. Of course, he might be spinning a line, but she somehow felt that he was sincere in needing her help.

"Could you slip out for ten minutes after dinner? I often take a stroll along the beach around ten o'clock. It's still warm then, and the bay is exquisite in moonlight." He gave her a pleading, sober look, pushing back his floppy fair hair with a brown hand.

He saw her expression stiffen, the doubt in her eyes, and added quickly, "Oh, I'm not setting up a romantic date! I have a girl of my own, and trouble enough without buying more by flirting with strangers!"

Claire felt again a prick of compassion. He had spoken with almost bitter seriousness.

"Well," she consented, "I'll try. But if I'm not there, don't wait too long."

Tony shrugged. "It won't matter if you are late. I have nothing else to do, and I really need some help. I wouldn't ask a girl normally, but you're English, and I'm sure I can make you understand." He took her hand, squeezing it. "Honestly, Claire, I'm at my wits' end. If you can't help me. . . ." and he shrugged, indicating total helplessness.

At that moment Claire became aware that a familiar sleek grey shape had pulled up beside them. Turning, she recognised the driver, with a sense of shock.

The passenger seat was empty, and the driver had

flung open the door on that side, and was leaning over to speak to them.

"Get in, Claire!"

Resenting his peremptory tone, yet unwilling to risk a scene in a public place, she obeyed. A few passers-by had already stopped to watch with interest.

Louis looked at Tony, his thin mouth compressed. "You are still here, I see, my friend! The sooner your lease is finished the better!"

Tony glared back, defiant yet uneasy, and did not answer. After a brief pause, the grey car shot ahead, and Claire sat back, seething.

For a while Louis drove in silence, his profile implacably aloof. Then he glanced at her and said coldly, "How did you meet that worthless idler? I suppose he scraped acquaintance with you somehow, and, being a female, you were taken in by his charm and good looks. You did not notice the weakness of his mouth or the lines which experience has carved on his face. It did not occur to you that he was an opportunist, a professional womaniser!"

"Tony may be weak," she said indignantly, "but I don't believe he's anything worse!"

His grey eyes glittered angrily. "You defend him! Were you flattered by his pursuit of you? I would not have said you were the sort of girl who likes to be accosted in a public place!"

"He spoke to me because I was English," she said quickly. "It was natural enough. He's a bit homesick. . . ."

"Homesick!" His voice rang with contempt. "That one is not capable of such an emotion! But the fact

47

that he is from your own country made his lack of moral qualities irrelevant, I suppose. Had you been so directly accosted by a Frenchman or an Italian, you would have walked away quickly. Ah, but this man is English! So you smiled at him and let him flatter you as much as he dared!"

"What right have you to be so insulting?" she demanded angrily. "I'm not a fool. I'm under no illusions about Tony, but, being English too, I saw things in him to which you are blind."

He smiled cynically. "Indeed? How fascinating. What, for instance?"

"I saw that he was a little frivolous, but basically with some sort of integrity. I wouldn't expect you to understand that. Tony may not be very reliable in some things, but I would trust him absolutely in others."

"Integrity!" The word exploded from his tight lips like a bomb. "He does not know the meaning of the word. I see that he had taken you in completely." He spun dangerously round a sharp bend and was silent for a moment. Then, harshly, "You will not meet him again! I will not have you exposed to such men as Kirk. You are too innocent to comprehend the extent of his folly."

They pulled up in the hotel car park and Claire slipped out of the car before he had time to come round to open the door for her. He caught her elbow as she walked towards reception.

"You resent my plain speaking!" His grey eyes held hers, icy and withdrawn. "I am only doing what any

48

responsible man would do to protect an innocent young girl who is under his protection!"

"I am not under your protection," she protested furiously. "I'm an adult, and can take care of myself!" Shaking free of his hold, she ran into the hotel, and was in the lift on her way upstairs before he could follow her.

She had brought one black dress with her, specifically for her first meeting with the Trebouls, since, although her father had decreed that they should not go into mourning for Paul, Claire felt that it would be misinterpreted by a French family if she did not make a gesture towards their customs of mourning. She knew that mourning was very much adhered to in parts of France and she did not want to hurt Madame Treboul.

When she joined Louis in the reception hall, she was glad that she had brought the black dress, since both Madame and Monsieur Treboul were in black. Madame stood, very upright, wearing a stark dress in black silk, with a high neckline and long sleeves. Her dark hair was wound in a thick coil upon the top of her head, her pale face only lightly made up. She had a strongly marked face, with a thin and dominating nose, slanting dark eyes and very heavy brows. Beside her, stooped and mild, her husband was insignificant, yet it was to him that Claire was drawn by the expression of sad resignation in his soft brown eyes.

As Claire came slowly towards them, feeling like a new girl on her first day at school, they stared at her with open and unreadable curiosity.

She trembled slightly and Louis stepped forward

to join her, looking sharply into her face, his hand gripping her arm. She found it inexpressibly comforting to feel his long, powerful fingers against the flimsy chiffon of her sleeves, their warmth penetrating to her cold skin.

"Here is our Claire," he said, his accent gently teasing. "Do you see a likeness, Armand, my dear friend? I confess I did not, at first, but now sometimes I see one in the turn of the head, the shape of the eyes. These family likenesses are elusive, no?"

Monsieur Treboul glanced at his wife, then stepped forward, holding out both hands. "We are glad to see you at last, Claire, although it is a sad occasion for a first meeting. We had hoped to see you long ago."

Claire bit her lip, quivering, and felt Louis's hand press her arm more firmly.

"Armand," he said in warm and rallying tones, "we shall not look back at the past today, eh? Claire is here, and we must make her welcome, so that she may think kindly of our France."

Monsieur Treboul smiled and nodded, then glanced, almost guiltily at his silent wife. She had been staring at Claire with hard, dark eyes, observing every inch of her, from her silky fair head to her small shoes, appraising the simple black dress with its scooped neckline and long sleeves and dismissing it with a flicker of her lashes.

Now she held out a limp, cold hand. "Welcome to St. Hilaire," she said in a frigid voice, touching Claire's hand without pressure.

Clearly, Claire thought, it would take a long time

before Madame Treboul forgave the members of the Stratton family for their long neglect of her daughter. Monsieur Treboul might one day be persuaded to forgive. His wife was a different case entirely.

Blandly, Louis moved them into the dining-room, talking with softly modulated charm to Madame while retaining his grip upon Claire, the thin fingers almost meeting around the slender arm.

The table was decorated tonight with a bowl of exquisite roses, an almost bluish white in the outer petals, with a few very pale pink petals in the centre. Their hearts were golden with thick pollen, and a few drops of water shone on their damask purity, as though they had been picked in the early morning with the dew still on them.

Louis glanced at them, then down at Claire, his grey eyes oddly intent. He courteously seated Madame on his right, Claire on his left, with Monsieur Treboul opposite himself. The waiter appeared, began to pour wine and serve a prearranged meal. They began with prawns, served in a nest of salad, then continued with steak, cooked at the table in a flambé sauce, and ended with a rich and delectable dessert of chocolate and rum whipped into cream and forming bland peaks beneath which the chef had hidden rum-impregnated pears.

Madame was served liberally and ate with silent concentration. She smiled at Louis as she laid down her spoon, her face almost happy.

"Excellent, my dear Louis. I wish I could persuade Pierre to give me that recipe. Every time I eat that I am amazed by the superb taste."

He smiled at her, inclining his head. "You are very kind. I shall see what I can do to persuade him. If you swear never to divulge the secret, he may be amenable."

Madame leaned back, smiling triumphantly. Louis glanced at her husband and raised one thin eyebrow. "I have been thinking, *mon cher*, that while Claire is with us, we might take a little trip to the Loire. It is unthinkable that she should go home without having seen our most beautiful landscapes."

"It is a long time since I saw Le Petit Trésor," Monsieur agreed eagerly. "Certainly, the English always like our chateaux."

"We must also see that our Claire learns a little French," Louis said calmly. "She will wish to speak it sufficiently to understand us better."

"What makes you think I don't speak French?" Claire spoke in his language, her voice a little sharp, forgetting her nervous fear of sounding foolish because of her irritation with him.

His brows rose. "So! Your accent is faulty, your pronunciation too stiff, but with practice you should improve!"

"How gracious of you!" She regretted the retort as she saw Madame stiffen in shocked surprise.

Curiously, it was Monsieur Treboul who lightened the atmosphere. Chuckling, he said, "It will be good for you, Louis, to have Claire to instruct you in the modern freedoms. Our young people do not so easily accept patronage, I find. They are eager to try their wings, to discover for themselves! It is admirable, I think, this bold defiance of authority. It takes courage, eh, Claire?" And his lined face twinkled humorously at her.

Louis leaned back, his lids lowered slightly, watching Claire from between his lashes. "There is little between courage and folly, Armand. But," gesturing tolerantly in a way which made Claire furious, "we will overlook Claire's childish independence. It is this peculiar mixture of wilful independence and lack of sophistication which makes the young English girls so baffling."

Armand Treboul nodded. "Yes, one sees them in their . . . what do you call them? Mini-skirts? One sees them and has an impression of permissive parents and wildness, but when one meets them one is amazed by their sensitivity and intelligence."

Madame looked extremely dubious, but said nothing, watching them all from darkly thoughtful eyes.

Claire's back was stiff with indignation. "I'm sure most French girls are just the same. The world is a very small place in the days of the moon rocket and the Common Market."

Louis laughed. "It is fashionable to say so, but in my experience it is a fallacy!" His glance challenged and mocked her. "Unlike you, my dear Claire, I have travelled widely, and I find each place very different."

She gave him a cold, wary glance. He looked extremely attractive, smiling teasingly across the table, but she did not trust him in this mood.

"They say beauty is in the eye of the beholder," she shrugged. "I suppose the same principle applies to other things. We all see what we want to see."

Monsieur Treboul laughed again, his eyes twinkling

from one to the other of them. "She has you there, my friend." he said in soft French.

Louis leaned forward, his hand very near Claire's on the table, his eyes holding hers. She felt suddenly uneasy, her heart beating up in her throat with suffocating urgency, her eyes unable to drop away from that dominating grey gaze.

"Sometimes," he said very softly, "young people are unable to see anything but their own prejudices."

"And that wouldn't apply to you, of course!" she retorted, escaping from her sense of his overwhelming presence by forcing herself to continue the argument. "Your own mind is as omniscient as God!"

He laughed, his eyes wrinkling. "How childish of you, my dear Claire! What is your English saying . . . sticks and stones may break my bones, but words can never harm me?"

Madame Treboul had listened to this exchange with a slowly congealing expression of distaste, and now, having finished her coffee, announced that she and her husband must be leaving.

Monsieur looked uncertainly at her, then at Claire. "You must visit us, my dear, very soon."

Claire flushed, looking at Madame with wide, appealing eyes. But the older woman said nothing, withdrawing from the room with rigid dignity, her husband scurrying after her like a frightened mouse.

Claire looked at Louis with tear-filled eyes, regardless of the other diners. "I hope you're satisfied, *monsieur*! You've probably ruined my chances of placating Madame Treboul! Why did you have to start that silly argument?" She pushed past him and almost ran out of the dining-room, stumbling against Monsieur Treboul on the way but not even noticing him, her sight was so blinded by the hot rush of tears.

In her room Claire sat down on one of the deep armchairs and dropped her head into her hand, weeping uncontrollably. She had been too busy nursing her father to have felt the full impact of Paul's death, but now, with her guard down, the tears seemed to be coming from a bottomless pit. She wept without knowing quite what she wept for, her body shaking like a leaf, all the pent-up emotions of the last few months released into violent expression.

She did not even hear the tap on her door, nor hear Louis enter after a moment's pause. The first she knew of his presence was when hands drew down the fingers pressed over her eyes, tilted up her drooping head, and began gently to wipe her face with a damp handkerchief.

She suffered it like a child, too exhausted by that storm of tears to have the strength to resist.

"That is enough," he said quietly. "You react too violently, child. A small setback should not have brought on such a scene as you played out in the dining-room!"

She flushed. "I ... I'm sorry. It means so much to me to make friends with Madame Treboul."

"Then you must go about it in a different way. Tomorrow you will be calm, polite and discreet. And I promise, I will not tease you into losing your temper."

She looked up hopefully, trembling a little. "Tomorrow?"

He inclined his head. "We take lunch with Madame at the Villa."

"Oh!" Claire was too joyful to be able to hide her relief, her still wet blue eyes shining up at him, her lips quivering upwards at the corners. His grey glance moved over her face, narrowed with some unreadable expression. For a brief, unbelievable second, she imagined that his face came down towards hers, his eyes on her parted lips. Then he was walking towards the door, bidding her good night in calm tones.

When he had gone she pressed her palms to her burning cheeks. What madness to think that Louis de Carceron would kiss her! She must be getting weak in the head even to dream such a thing.

She stood up and glanced at the clock. Should she go out and meet Tony, as she had promised? She felt too worn out to consider it, but then she remembered the urgency of his request. If he was really in trouble she ought to do what she could for him. It must be frightening to be alone in a foreign country and need a friend. Suppose it had happened to Paul!

She found a stole, wrapped it around her shoulders, and went back down to reception, hoping desperately that she would not meet Louis again. He would be bound to ask awkward questions.

Fortunately there was no sign of him, although the desk clerk did look across rather curiously as she slipped out into the warm night.

She found Tony at the top of the beach steps, smoking a cigarette whose red tip glowed in the darkness like a beacon.

He lifted a casual hand in greeting as she joined

him, gesturing to the low wall which served him as a
seat, and Claire sat down, gazing out over the moonlit
sea with dreamy eyes.

"Thanks for coming," Tony said soberly. "I hope
Louis didn't see you."

"I don't think so, but I mustn't stay too long. What
did you want to talk about?"

He dropped his cigarette and trod it carefully into
the gravel before replying. "I don't know quite where
to start. You're so damned young."

Claire groaned. "Oh, don't say it! I'm sick
of hearing how young I am! I wish I could wear a
placard saying I'm over twenty-one and quite capable
of living my own life!"

He laughed. "Well, it is a bit complicated. You see,
when I came here I was only intending to stay a few
months, but I met this girl."

She chuckled. "Famous last words! And you fell
in love?"

"I didn't mean to," he said regretfully. "She isn't
even my type. She's dark, and clever. I didn't know
what had hit me. The trouble is her family. Her father
wants her to marry someone else—an arranged match.
It sounds very suitable." His voice was bitter. "He's
wealthy and of good family. The fact that Marise
doesn't love him makes no difference, it seems."

Claire regarded him sympathetically. "I'm very
sorry, Tony. But what can I do? I couldn't possibly
attempt to interfere."

"I don't want you to," he said quickly. "Marise has
refused to consider marrying this other chap. But even
then our problems don't end, because her father would

never agree to an engagement between us. I'm penniless, and I don't even have a steady job. That's where you come in. . . ."

"Me?" Claire laughed, then sobered. "I'm sorry, Tony, but I'm afraid I couldn't help you there, either. I have no influential contacts in your world."

"You know Louis," he said simply.

She turned her head to stare at him. "Louis?"

Tony leaned forward eagerly. "I've been living on my savings so far and I'm completely broke. I can't earn enough for two people by writing the occasional article. But I have an idea for a book. To do it properly I need personal introductions. That's where Louis comes in, Claire. He can help me by giving me letters to various people. There's no use in my applying to him myself—he would just refuse."

"Have you tried?"

He shook his head. "I haven't dared. He hates the sight of me. You saw how he was when he met us in town today. And if he found out about Marise he would have me pushed back to England."

"You mean her family don't know about you?"

"She says there would be no point. They would just make sure we didn't meet again. I give her English lessons once a week and we sometimes manage to meet in town." He grimaced. "Believe me, Claire, love that can feed on such brief contact must be something special." He sighed. "I'm crazy about her. If I lose her, I lose everything. I've got to get a steady job, and the only sort of job I've ever considered is a job on a London newspaper, as their travel expert."

She nodded. "It sounds interesting!"

"If I write this book, I'll have a chance of getting such a job. I know a couple of people in London, and I have a strong hope of being offered a job on a Sunday paper. I could still travel, but I would be based in London, and Marise and I could marry."

"What's your book about?" she asked.

"Historic houses in France," he said with an enthusiastic grin. "Houses that are still privately owned but have an exciting story to them. Like the Petit Trésor.... I would certainly want to use that! I expect you know all about it. Now, Louis knows all these people. He could get me into their homes. I know that without some sort of backing I would get no co-operation at all."

Claire was silent for a moment, thinking hard. She suspected that Louis would be difficult to persuade, yet how could she refuse to help Tony? His story was so romantic and sad. And his face was in such deadly earnest that she could not doubt his sincerity.

"Will you approach Louis for me, Claire?" he asked.

"I'll do my best," she said slowly. "Now I must go."

He walked back with her, and as they came near the hotel, took her hand. "I shall be eternally grateful, Claire, and so will Marise! I'd like you to meet her. We must arrange it, somehow."

"I would like that," she said gently. "Is she very pretty?"

He was silent, grinning crookedly. "Pretty? Well, no, not exactly. But she can look beautiful at times."

The answer moved her, and she smiled up at him,

squeezing his hand. "You really do love her, don't you?"

"Like hell," he said grimly. "I always thought of love as something sweet and gay, but believe me, Claire, it can be murder. I get desperate at times, when I think of losing Marise."

She left him a moment later, took the lift up to her suite, and halted at the door, staring at it in bewilderment. Had she left it open when she left? No, she could remember locking it behind her.

Nervously she pushed it wider and saw a man standing at the opposite side of the sitting-room, by the window, his shoulders blocking the pale shaft of moonlight.

He moved round very slowly and looked at her across the darkened room.

Her heart plunged violently. It was Louis. Had he seen her with Tony? Why was he here?

CHAPTER FOUR

THE taut silence between them stretched her nerves unbearably. When he did not move or speak, she plunged into stammered excuses, growing increasingly bothered as she went on speaking.

"I ... I was taking a walk ... before turning in. I couldn't get to sleep and it was so ... so ... mild. ..."

When she had stammered herself into silence again there was another long pause. His face was still in shadow, but she could distinguish the glitter of his eyes. Alarm bells were ringing wildly in her head. What was he thinking? Why didn't he say something? He must have seen her with Tony! He was angry, shocked by her behaviour. They were far more strict with girls in France, of course. It was hard to remember that. At home her father would think nothing if she took a walk at midnight, through the dark fields down to the cliffs, except perhaps to complain that she would be tired next morning.

She knew that if nothing happened soon she would scream, so she moved to the side and switched on the light, blinking after the darkness. Then she walked across the room, evading his gaze, dropped her stole on a chair and stood, like a shamed child, head bent, hands plaited together, waiting for him to speak.

Louis leaned against the window-frame, arms folded, watching her, still saying nothing. Anger began to burn in Claire. What was this? A new form of torture?

She lifted her head suddenly, hearing him move. He had straightened and was crossing to her. She was painfully conscious of the powerful, broad shoulders, the arrogantly held head. He stood within a hand's distance, staring fixedly at her.

"Who was it out there with you? Kirk?"

Claire swallowed, raising her eyes to meet his in a collision that knocked all the breath out of her body. She nodded without speaking, afraid to trust her voice.

"You agreed to meet him furtively at such an hour, in a lonely spot where there would be no one to help you if you needed help?" He spoke slowly, with icy restraint, yet she was nervously aware that behind the controlled voice something else leapt, something she did not understand, yet which filled her with an indefinable sense of menace.

"We've had this argument before," she said hurriedly. "I've told you, my father wouldn't put me through such a catechism. Why should I put up with it from a stranger?"

His voice grew harder. "Do not tell me your father would approve of you meeting a man like Kirk alone at night! I will not believe it. No father could permit such a folly."

"My father would not have allowed me to come to France had he not thought me capable of looking after myself!"

He moved restlessly, with a violent twist of the shoulders, as though shaking something off, then began to pace the room, speaking swiftly. "I cannot believe that you are normally so free in your behaviour with strangers! What is it about Kirk that women find so attractive?"

Claire laughed nervously. "You don't understand. . . ."

His dark swift glance alarmed her, and she stepped back, plaiting her fingers again. His eyes reminded her of the sea at Trevillion, crashing savagely against the rocks, as though it would willingly destroy them. Why did he detest Tony so much? Was it possible that he had, after all, some inkling of Tony's relationship with this girl Marise? Did Louis, perhaps, have more than a friendly interest in Marise? Tony had not named the man whom Marise's parents wished her to marry, but it might be Louis. It would explain the tension between them.

She swallowed. "Please believe me, nothing happened out at the beach that I wouldn't wish my father to have seen! Tony and I talked, that's all."

"And held hands!" His voice was savage with distaste. "Do not deny it! I saw you from this window. I rang you to make arrangements for our visit to the Trebouls and was alarmed when there was no reply, so I came up to your suite. I was just about to begin a search for you when I saw you with Kirk, coming back to the hotel." His lips thinned. "I wonder what else I might have seen had I been there earlier!"

"Nothing! There was nothing to see!" Claire was hotly angry now, infuriated by the malicious innuendo. Searching for some weapon with which to hit back, she said tartly, "It seems to me less compromising for me to go for a walk in the dark with Tony than it is being alone here with you now!" She glared at him, expecting to see him taken aback.

To her surprise the grey eyes widened and an odd little smile moved the corners of his mouth. "You feel uneasy alone with me, Claire? I have noticed how your eyes evade mine, how you quiver and look disturbed. I thought your guilt caused these symptoms, but is it possible that some other emotion has been at work?"

A pulse began to beat at her temple, she felt a strange trembling in the pit of her stomach. The conceit of the man! Was he implying that she was . . . attracted to him? Her eyes flashed.

"It may seem strange to you, *monsieur*, but I have a rooted objection to being cross-questioned all the time. You must be a branch of the Spanish Inquisition!"

His face altered, he turned away, thrusting his hands into his pockets. "It is late. We will discuss this tomorrow. I shall be ready to leave for the Villa Treboul at ten o'clock tomorrow. I thought you might like to visit our famous windmill church on the way. It is a popular tourist attraction."

She nodded. "Thank you, *monsieur*."

He threw her an irritated, quizzical glance. "Do you not think you could bring yourself to call me Louis?"

"I'm sorry—Louis."

Louis sighed. "Good night, Claire. No more nocturnal rambling, eh?"

She smiled. "I'm very tired. I shall go to bed at once."

He nodded. "Excellent! Then I may retire with an easy mind!"

When he had gone she got ready for bed and curled up, her thoughts still too active for sleep. Talking to Louis seemed to have become a series of fencing bouts, each more dangerous than the last. Tonight she had been distinctly aware of danger emanating from him, although she could not quite pin down her intuition. That he had been very angry had been plain. What she had not decided was—why?

She must ask Tony when they next met if it had been Louis whom Marise's family had wanted her to marry. She twisted uneasily. It was none of her business, of course, what Louis felt. He was an aggravating, impossible man, his temper as deadly as a stiletto. She disliked him more than any man she had ever met.

Next morning she came down to see him talking to a woman in the hotel entrance, his hand resting intimately on her shoulder, his head bent in an attitude of charming attention. Claire recognised her at once. It was the woman she had seen with him on that first day. She watched them curiously, wondering who the woman was, and what was engrossing their attention. They were too intent on each other to notice anyone or anything else.

Suddenly Louis bent his head in a foreign gesture and kissed the woman's ungloved hand lightly. Claire felt a sharp pang, and again those alarm bells rang in her head, this time much more loudly. Why should it matter to her that Louis had kissed that woman's hand? It must be the unsettling nature of her new surroundings which made her emotions so volatile and unpredictable.

When she glanced back towards the entrance, the woman had gone, and Louis was moving towards her.

Claire gave him a bright, hard smile. "I'm ready."

His eyes probed hers, a frown creasing his forehead, but he said nothing. A few moments later they were driving out of the town and towards the hazy blue peaks which stood up against the summer sky.

Claire stared out of the window, aware of the silence between them yet relieved not to have to talk. The road was lined with villas, set in gardens ablaze with all manner of flowers and umbrella pines casting deep shadows on smooth lawns. Few other cars passed them. The dusty road shone like a silver ribbon, curling round a hill studded with olive trees and cypress. The bright flashing of other windscreens signalled the approach of other vehicles further up the hill.

Looking back as they took one of the bends, she caught a glimpse of the town, picturesque roofs huddled together, pink and green, wavy with age, especially in the fishing harbour area, where the streets were particularly narrow and closely packed with old houses. Beyond the town sparkled the bay, a vivid postcard blue, glittering in the sunshine and gay with little yachts with coloured sails, which seemed as tiny as toys from this height.

She was surprised when Louis pulled off the road

and took a bumpy cart track beneath the shadowy trees. He glanced sideways.

"This leads to the windmill church," he explained.

"Why is it called that?"

"You will see."

The car jolted to a stop, throwing her forward, and Louis caught at her in time to stop her hitting her head on the windscreen.

"I am sorry," he said, with concern. "I was taking it too fast."

Claire laughed, a little breathless, aware of his arm around her. "No harm done!"

"There might have been!" He gestured towards the seat belt hanging behind her. "I should have noticed that you had not put that on. You must always do so." His hand delicately touched her cheek. "It would be a tragedy to spoil this face!"

Claire blushed and moved uneasily away from him.

Louis got out, walked round and assisted her to alight. His hand slipped under her elbow. "The track is very uneven," he said in explanation. "You must watch your step."

They walked through a belt of the usual pines, through pools of dark shadow which were coolly refreshing after the glare of the sun outside, and emerged on a hillside. Above them rose a strange building, half church, half windmill, the rough grey stones seeming to have been thrown up out of the rock beneath the grass.

"Long ago, the priest of this church was a farmer, too. He had to supplement his income somehow, so he built a windmill at the side of his church here, and ground the corn for the local peasants, as well as his own. For some reason, it has never been rebuilt, and now it is such an attraction that I doubt if it ever will be."

"It's very remote," Claire said, gazing down over the green valley. There were very few houses to be seen.

"There is a village on the other side of the hill, but it is a small one, and the church has a small congregation." He shrugged. "Have you seen enough, or shall we go up there?"

"We ought to go," Claire decided reluctantly. "Is it far to the Villa?"

"No, not now," he said calmly. "We will stop for coffee at the café further on."

They drove on up the road until Louis pulled up beside a small, white-painted café and led her to one of the tables outside, over which a red and white umbrella fluttered gently.

They were the only customers. The owner hurried out eagerly to serve them, recognised Louis and burst into polite French. Louis ordered, smiling, and when the man had withdrawn, looked at Claire across the table with a cool smile.

"And now ... we have something to discuss, I think?"

She started, eyes opening wide, then sighed. It was peaceful here, perched on the side of this wooded hill, the only sound the sighing of the breeze in the pine trees, the air sweet with gentle scents of rosemary and thyme. It seemed a pity to spoil such a moment.

68

He seemed to read her thoughts. "You would rather postpone our discussion?"

She looked appealingly at him, her pale hair blowing back from her face, the dark blue eyes huge.

"It's very peaceful here, isn't it?"

He raised a teasing eyebrow. "So! You like our mountains. I am glad there is something you like!"

"I'm not difficult to please. It's just that Trevillion. . . ."

"Ah!" He smiled wryly, lighting a cigarette. "One day I must see this Trevillion. It must be a wonderful place. You use it as a yardstick for everything else you see, and always it outshines them in your opinion."

"It isn't a pretty place," she said, her eyes dreamily fixed on the blue haze of the mountains behind them, which always seemed to be the same distance away although they had now covered several miles. "It's wild and stormy, set on the rocks above the sea, but when once you've grown used to the sound of the wind blowing through the thorn trees, and have heard the sea dashing against the rocks, you never seem to drive the sound from your head!"

He watched her intently. "Thorn trees?" he questioned. "What are they?"

"Trevillion is very exposed. Trees don't grow well there. The only ones that survive are thorn trees, and they're salt-blighted and twisted in shape."

He laughed. "A grim spot! Yet you prefer it to the beauty of St. Hilaire, which is famous!"

His derisive tone stung. "Trevillion is grim," Claire admitted defiantly. "But there's something triumphant about it, too. Life hangs on there, with great difficulty, and I think human beings have to fight, if life is to be worthwhile. I would hate to find life too easy. It makes one soft."

"You consider life at St. Hilaire soft? Have you seen the faces of our old people? Wrinkled with toil and poverty!"

She nodded. "They don't stay at the Hotel St. Hilaire, though, do they?"

Dark red crept up beneath his tan. "So! We come to it! Ever since you arrived you have been silently critical of the hotel. You have been nowhere, seen nothing, yet you stare at the hotel and the other guests with the censorious eyes of a nun plunged into an orgy! I thought at first it was because you had inherited your father's dislike of the French, but it becomes clear that you have stronger motives. You despise the wealthy guests because they have had easier lives than yours!"

"My father doesn't dislike the French," she said hotly. "And I don't despise your guests!"

He shrugged. "Your protests are rather unconvincing!"

There was a pause as the owner served them with a pot of coffee, hot and fragrant, and two cups which matched the pot, sturdily gay in a bright orange earthenware. Claire hesitated, then poured the coffee, while Louis watched her.

During the silence in which they sipped their coffee, she became aware of a strange little sound, insistent and repetitive, which had been present since they arrived, but which she only now consciously noticed. When she asked him, he looked surprised. "That is the

70

cicadas. Have you never heard them before? They are like one's conscience, rasping away, harsh and impossible to silence! I think they are most like your English crickets."

She laughed. "It's a monotonous sound! But it fits the surroundings."

"Like your wind through the thorn trees?" His glance was intimate. "It is odd that you should enjoy the struggle life on your stark rock imposes."

"Odd? Why?"

"You have such a feminine appearance," he said flatly, with an indifference that piqued her. "That blonde hair, the delicate features. . . ." He suddenly sat up and snapped his fingers. "I have it!"

Claire jumped at the abrupt exclamation, staring at him.

His eyes were alight. "I knew you were familiar to me. Even in the photographs Paul showed me . . . a tantalising resemblance which I could not place . . . you are the lady with the unicorn!"

She stared in bewilderment.

"You do not know it?" he demanded eagerly. "Have you never seen a photograph of a tapestry showing a medieval girl with a unicorn? If you wore your hair pulled back from your face, and a wimple, leaving exposed these delicate fine bones of yours, you would be the image of the girl. It is our most famous tapestry. It is in the museum of Cluny. You should go there one day." He leaned back, smiling, pleased with himself. "I am glad I thought of it at last! The resemblance had been teasing me for years."

She was curious. So Paul had shown him

71

photographs of her? She remembered sending her brother some snaps taken by her father last summer, of her with Peter Dillon, laughing and untidy on top of a rock. They had been picnicking on the beach and Peter had pretended to threaten her with a piece of seaweed. It seemed strange to look back at that day. There had been some tension between herself and Peter. He had been nervous, guilty, a little shamefaced because of his surrender to his mother's possessive jealousy. She had been determined to prove he had not hurt her. It all seemed rather futile now, all that soul-searching. She knew that she had never been in love with Peter and the slight sting of wounded pride he had caused her had been merely a rehearsal for . . .

She sat up stiffly. What was she thinking of? Her cheeks burnt a bright angry red and she whipped her errant thoughts into line, becoming aware that Louis was regarding her with narrowed eyes.

"I'm sorry," she stammered. "Did you say something?"

"You were deep in other thoughts," he said evenly. "First you smiled, then you sighed, then you looked angry. If I were a mind-reader I would hazard a guess that your thoughts concerned a man." He smiled tormentingly. "But of course, that is out of the question! You are too young to feel any serious emotion."

"Am I?" She felt a hot, stifling emotion fill her now, and hoped it did not show in her face. Troubling thoughts, it seemed, were to dominate her mind whether she liked it or not. It must be the warm romantic air of St. Hilaire!

They lapsed into silence again. He smoked a cigarette, staring into the cloudless sky with narrowed eyes. Claire leaned back, the harshly beautiful chant of the cicadas making her drowsy, the warmth and silence of this lovely place seeping into her mind as the heat of the sun permeated every part of her body.

When Louis spoke it woke her out of her dream, and she opened her eyes reluctantly, their lids sun-warm, to find the dazzle of the light blinding.

"Now!" He leaned forward, holding her eyes. "What were you talking to Kirk about last night? Why did you meet him? I have put off the discussion long enough."

Well, she thought, it had to come, sooner or later. She had promised Tony to do what she could for him and Marise, and she meant to keep her word.

Nervously she began to explain Tony's position, his lack of money, his desire to take a job in England, his lack of suitable qualifications unless he wrote a book which would sell and make his name as a travel writer. Louis listened without interruption, but she was aware that he tensed and looked angry from time to time. Carefully she explained Tony's need of introductions, his idea of writing a book about privately owned historic houses in France.

She finished hastily by admitting that it was Louis's help he required, and saw the brooding face blaze into rage.

"*Ciel!* He is impudent. You mean to tell me that this philandering Englishman has the insolence to ask me to introduce him to my friends? To recommend them to accept him as a trustworthy person whom

73

they may safely admit to their homes? *Mon Dieu*, he must think me a fool!"

"He only wants to write about their homes, not become part of their social life," she said indignantly. "You make him sound dishonest!"

"What else? You admit that he is in debt, that he owes so much money that he is desperate to find a way out! Is it not dishonest to borrow money you know you cannot repay?"

"He means to pay those debts, though," she said quickly. "Why else would he want to write this book? And he can't visit these houses unless he's vouched for by someone. . . ." She paused, not sure how to go on.

Louis finished for her. "Someone more trustworthy than himself? Well, I will not do it! My own good name would be at stake, and I would not trust this . . ." he fumed, then said, "this scoundrel!"

"That's going too far," snapped Claire, firing up. "Tony is weak, I grant you, but he's not a scoundrel!"

He stared at her. "Why are you asking me this? Why did he not come to me himself?"

"He knows you dislike him!"

His mouth twisted. "Perceptive of him! But he understates the case, as the English so often do, I find. I detest him!" The savagery in his voice made her wince. She was becoming increasingly certain that Louis had some personal reason for his attitude to Tony. Was it jealousy? Had he proposed for Marise because he loved her? She wondered what Marise was like, this girl who had inspired deep love in a man as rootless as Tony Kirk. And, possibly, in Louis de Carceron, too.

74

Calmly, she said aloud, "Tony is quite pleasant, you know."

"Pleasant!" His ejaculation was abrupt. "I find you incomprehensible! You prefer the wild coast of Cornwall to our charming St. Hilaire, yet you claim to find Kirk pleasant. He is weak, selfish and idle, yet you like him! Ask yourself—how would he fit your precious Trevillion? What sort of figure would he cut there?"

Claire smiled, her eyes amused. "He wouldn't fit at all," she admitted. And a strange thought struck her. Louis, for all his elegant worldliness, would fit better into the stormy backcloth of Trevillion. She had seen Cornishmen with dark faces like his, perhaps descended from the Spanish sailors of myth and legend, who had been thrown on to the Cornish coast during the flight of the Armada. She stared at him, seeing him suddenly in a new light, imagining him clad in the silks of an earlier age, a sword at his side, fighting his way up the dark Cornish beaches.

Their eyes suddenly met, hers wide and dreamy, his sharp and full of dislike.

He leaned forward, his hands on the table. "Are you in love with Kirk?" The question shot at her like a bullet from a gun, and she reeled back from the shock before spontaneously bursting into laughter.

"Of course not! I only met him yesterday!" Although, she admitted privately, it seemed far longer.

"You do not believe in love at first sight?" His voice was curiously flat as though he were repressing something.

"I don't know," she said lightly. "I've never experienced it!"

75

"Have you *ever* been in love?"

Panic gripped her suddenly. She wanted to get away from him, away from these probing questions, the sharp shrewd grey eyes which watched her relentlessly. "We're getting rather personal," she said, forcing a smile. "What has this to do with Tony's problem?"

He shrugged. "I was merely curious. You have . . ." he hesitated, "an untouched look. I suspected you had had no experience of love, and I am glad to find I was right."

"I didn't say I hadn't been in love!"

"You did not need to! It was in your face." He called the owner, paid the bill and assisted her back into the car. When he was seated beside her, his hands on the wheel, the long fingers gripping it desultorily, he glanced at her with mocking grey eyes.

"Your face is a blank page, Claire. When love has written there, we shall see a new softness to your lips, a new look in your eyes. It is unmistakable, that expression. It tells of pain, of hope, of a sweetness unrealised." His voice was low and intimate, his smile a little tormenting. "You are a girl at the moment. When love has touched your face you will be a woman."

Claire's heart beat suffocatingly. She could not look away from him.

Then, with one of those odd changes of mood which baffled her, he glanced away and said, "Give me the list Kirk gave you. I will see to it, but you must give me your word never to speak to him again."

"I can't do that!"

"Why not? You have said you do not love him."

"What if I meet him in the town? I can't ignore him!"

"You will be polite but evasive," he said. "As you often are with me! You will know how to handle it, I am sure."

She handed him the list which she had in her handbag, and he pushed it into an inner pocket, then drove back on to the road and continued up the hill.

The Villa Treboul lay a mile off, set among lawns and flowers, with two dark cypresses guarding the gates, and a striped garden swing standing in the shade of a lemon tree.

They lunched in a sunny, spacious room, with windows opening on to a lawn, and the sound of birds echoing from the garden.

Madame Treboul was not unfriendly today. She maintained a courteous flow of conversation on general topics, but the one subject which Claire longed to discuss never came up. She was dying to ask about Jean-Paul and Marie-Claire, and could not help speculating on which rooms they inhabited when they were living at the villa, but Louis's eyes were constantly upon her, willing her silently to follow Madame's lead.

Monsieur Treboul was gently attentive, but when they all returned back to the small drawing-room at the front of the villa, he grew sleepy and gradually dropped into a light doze, his head resting on the back of his chair. Madame glanced at him, her face softening as she took in his parted lips, the drooped lips and relaxed limbs.

Claire's gaze was on a small bureau on which stood

a framed photograph she recognised. It was of the two children, taking a donkey ride at some resort in France, their parents holding the reins and smiling at them. Paul had sent her a copy in one of his last letters, and she had shown it to her father, watching eagerly as his face grew stiff with pain and yearning. But he had stubbornly turned away, fighting down his natural feelings, and she had left the photograph on his desk. He had put it somewhere, she supposed, but she had never heard him mention it since.

Claire's eyes filled with tears as she saw it again. How young and happy Paul and Madeleine looked! And how pretty Marie-Claire was, with her baby face and frilly sunbonnet, her fat dimpled arms stretched out to her mother. Jean-Paul was intent on touching the donkey's long ears, his tongue protruding from his mouth, his eyes screwed up against the sun. They had been such a happy little family!

Madame's voice broke in on her thoughts. "Yes, that is your brother and my daughter with their two little ones!" The tone was harsh and broken, and Claire looked quickly at her.

The stolid dark eyes were glistening with sternly suppressed tears. The heavy face was contorted with bitter emotion. Forgetting everything else, Claire instinctively rose and went to her, kneeling beside her chair, touching the tensed hands gently, with shy compassion.

"I know! It hurts! Paul was very dear to me. I can't . . . can't. . . ." Her voice broke, but she went on with determination. "I can't believe he's dead! It's like a bad dream! I had looked forward to coming here to France, to meeting Madeleine at last . . . I had learned French so that I could talk to her in her own language. . . . I had planned it so many times . . . and now, never. . . ." She buried her head against Madame's chair, sobbing.

The stiff fingers moved convulsively, touched her pale head. Madame bit her lip, stared down at the soft flood of silky hair lying spread over her lap.

"Hush," she said gently. "Hush, *ma petite*." And her hands stroked the fair hair, patted Claire's shoulder clumsily.

Louis had risen to his feet when Claire burst into tears, and now stood watching them with a shuttered expression on his dark countenance.

"I couldn't hurt my father by disobeying him," Claire whispered huskily. "I was caught between two people I love. I had the choice of either hurting Paul, or hurting my father. I knew Paul had Madeleine and the children. My father had no one but me. I had no right to desert him, even though he was wrong. I begged him to relent many times. I showed that photograph to him, hoping it would touch him. It did! I know it did! He looked so sad, yet he was still too proud to give in . . . even though he bitterly regretted it every day."

"Ah, pride!" Madame sighed thickly. "It is of the devil! They do not call it one of the seven deadly sins for nothing!" She lifted Claire by the shoulders and smiled shyly at her. One hand came up to brush back the tousled hair.

"*Ma chère*, you are a gentle child. Paul said that he did not envy you, shut up with your proud papa in that lonely place, and I see now that you have the tender heart, obedient as is fitting in a daughter. I am sorry if I have been unkind to you. I, too, was bitter with pride. I blamed the wrong person. Will you forgive me?"

"There's nothing to forgive," Claire said softly. "I knew, and understood, just as I understand my poor father. Love can make one do strange things."

Louis came up suddenly and jerked her to her feet, with an almost violent hand. "Come, we must be less emotional, no? Now you comprehend each other, all is well. No more tears or sadness!"

Madame looked past Claire and studied him with a puzzled expression. He was holding Claire's elbow, his fingers tight and compelling.

Claire looked down at the other woman, dark blue eyes wide and pleading. "But the children? When will I see the children?"

Madame folded her hands. "They will come home tomorrow, I think." She nodded. "Yes, they will come home tomorrow, certainly!"

Claire's mouth trembled into a smile of delight. She looked up at Louis eagerly. "Isn't it wonderful? I'm so happy!"

His face did not respond. Brooding, absorbed, he seemed almost not to hear her, with his grey eyes set on something in the distant sky and his mouth a firm, hard line.

CHAPTER FIVE

MADAME Treboul had decreed that Claire would meet her nephew and niece at the Villa so that they might have time to readjust to their surroundings.

"But they're so young," Claire pointed out to Louis. "Will they understand who I am?"

He had shrugged. "A new face, another personality to which they must become accustomed! They will not understand more than that."

"Jean-Paul is four now," Claire said, sighing. "He may remember something."

"Certainly, his father would have mentioned you to him," Louis agreed.

They were on their way back to the Villa, on the following afternoon, and Claire was in a state of extreme emotional and nervous tension. She had hardly slept, her thoughts in turmoil. She had written to her father, a short joyful note, and in her delight had mentioned Louis, the mediator who had arranged this happy ending, adding a brief but revealing portrait of him. It had taken her some time to express her view of his character, since she wished to be fair but felt that the conflict between them might have warped her attitude.

This afternoon Louis was different, although Claire could not put her finger on what change had occurred. He seemed more relaxed, more talkative. She thought that perhaps he was relieved to have successfully bridged the gap between herself and the Trebouls. He was the sort to take such a duty seriously.

She was surprised when he stopped at the same roadside café and came round to open her door and assist her to alight, with punctilious courtesy.

He read her expression and smiled lightly. "You are far too tense to meet the children yet. We shall take a leisurely tea here. You must make yourself wind down. You are like a piece of stretched elastic—one ounce of pressure and you would snap!"

It was sensible, she knew that, and acknowledged it with a faintly apologetic glance.

They sat sipping cups of straw-coloured tea, listening to the cicadas and the whispering of the wind in the trees. Claire felt her tension draining away, her bones relaxing slowly.

When they finally drew up outside the Villa she was able to greet Madame Treboul with a calm smile, drawing a look of approval from the heavy, dark face.

Still they had to go through the routine procedure of courtesy. Another tea was served, in the little drawing-room, on a round, polished walnut table. Louis passed Claire a fragile bone china cup, painted with roses of an incredible pink. With a sigh, she accepted a tiny cake, a fluted madeleine, which made her eyes quiver, the milky lids hurriedly descend to hide the unbidden glint of tears. Had Madame deliberately ordered madeleines for tea? No, it must be fortuitous, an unfortunate stroke of chance.

Louis stood between her and Madame, bending over her with a sugar bowl, his watchful eyes relentlessly probing the lowered curves of her face. Deftly, under cover of handing her sugar, he wiped her eyes with his handkerchief, which vanished again, as swiftly as if he were a conjuror, as he turned back to Madame.

"When shall we take our trip to the Loire?" he asked the other woman, smiling upon her with all his charm.

She spread her hands, the stiff knuckles hooped with rings. "I shall leave that to you, Louis. Are you inviting anyone else?"

"I have not taken visitors to Le Petit Trésor since last Christmas," he shrugged. "Too many people descending upon her might upset my poor Agathe!" He turned back to Claire, his glance taking in her bright smile, noting the pallor of her cheeks. "Agathe is my housekeeper. She was my nurse when I was a child."

"I . . . I have a very limited time at my disposal," Claire said anxiously. "I must get back to my father, you know."

"I understood that your sister was with him?" His brows drew together.

"Yes, Annette has a month's leave, but she's not fond of the country. I'm afraid she will get bored with looking after the house."

"Bored with Trevillion? Surely not!" His tone was openly mocking, but not unkind.

She smiled. "Annette is a city dweller. She's not at home in the country."

"And you? Have you never thought of living in a city?"

Claire shook her head. "I've never lived anywhere but Trevillion."

"And you would not like to?"

"I don't know," she admitted. "I've never had the chance to find out. I had to stay at home."

His regard was insistent. "You feel a faint resentment, perhaps?"

She flushed, shaking her head. "That's too strong a word. I've wondered if I might like other places, too. But I don't think I resent having had to stay at home. I suppose we all like to experiment."

"Especially when we are young," Madame nodded, in surprising approval. "Youth is the time for experiment."

"Well," Louis said, "Claire shall have the opportunity to see more of France when we drive up to the Loire. It will make it more interesting, perhaps, Madame, if we take several others with us. Marise has expressed a desire to see Le Petit Trésor."

Claire felt a jolt. Marise! So Louis *was* interested in her! Was he hoping to detach her from Tony?

Madame smiled. "Marise! Yes, that would be most suitable. Perhaps also her sister and Jacques? It has been so kind of them to look after the children for us." She turned to Claire, her dark eyes friendly. "Marie and Jacques Delmain are cousins of mine. It is they who have been caring for Jean-Paul and Marie-Claire this week. They have three children of their own. Marie Delmain was one of Marie-Claire's godparents." She smiled, her head inclining. "You, of course, were the other, my dear." She waved a hand. "I stood proxy for you at the ceremony, since you could not be present. It was Paul's wish."

Claire remembered only too well.

Louis intervened, "I seem to remember, Claire, you sent a charming silver bowl as a christening present."

She nodded. She had chosen it with such care, hoping to propitiate the Trebouls by showing that she valued her brother's suggestion, even though she could not come.

Madame gave Louis a fond look. "And you, *mon cher*, gave little Jean-Paul a handsome set of mugs, each bigger than the other, and engraved with his initials and date of birth. A beautiful heirloom for the child!"

Claire had finished her tea and, somehow, the madeleine too, and Madame rose slowly.

"Now, we shall go up to see the children." She nodded to Louis. "You will accompany us, *mon cher*?"

He smiled, taking Claire's arm in one thin hand. "I shall certainly do so! We godparents must show a united front!"

Madame led them upstairs and along a carpeted corridor to a white-painted door behind which Claire could hear the soft chirpings of a baby voice.

Madame knocked and entered. The room was sunny, with high, wide windows, the walls covered with a gay flowered wallpaper. Seated on the floor, running a lorry full of wooden bricks back and forth, was a small boy in blue shorts and a white cotton shirt. A young girl, her body enveloped in a huge white apron, sat on a low chair, nursing a small girl in a smocked pink dress.

"*Bonjour*, Jean-Paul. *Bonjour*, Marie-Claire!" Madame spoke with cheerful ease, not betraying by a flicker that anything unusual was happening.

Claire quivered, and Louis's hand tightened on her arm. She swallowed hard, willing herself to remain calm. She must not show any emotion. She must be quite ordinary.

"*Mon parrain! Mon parrain!*" Jean-Paul leapt up and flung himself at Louis, clutching his hands and dancing up and down.

Parrain, Claire guessed, must mean godfather, although she had not met the word before.

"Softly, softly," Louis smiled, lifting the boy up effortlessly, so that his head swooped up into the air, almost touching the ceiling. He lowered him to the floor again, laughing.

"Again! Again!" Jean-Paul giggled.

"Where are your manners?" Louis turned him towards Claire.

She smiled, holding herself steady by an effort. "*Bonjour*, Jean-Paul. *Ça va?*"

He stared, brown eyes round and curious. "You talk like my papa! I have seen pictures of you, I am sure."

"I am your Aunt Claire," she said, in slow French. "Your papa was my brother."

"*Ma tante?*" He looked up at Louis. "Is it true? She is my aunt?"

Louis nodded, watching them both.

The boy held out one small brown hand. Claire took it, fighting down the impulse to kiss him, wondering if he would be insulted if she treated him as a baby and took him in her arms.

"That is Marie-Claire," he said importantly, pointing at the little girl who was kicking her legs against her nurse's lap and watching them.

Madame picked up Marie-Claire and brought her to the other little group, handing her gently into Claire's open arms.

"Hallo, baby," Claire said softly, touching the petal cheek with one finger.

Marie-Claire had bright blue eyes, cheeks like flowers and a broad, happy smile. Her silky brown hair hung in ringlets to her ears. She wriggled in her aunt's arms, trying to grasp a lock of Claire's long hair.

"Françoise, come with me!" Madame went to the door, looked back at Claire. "I shall be ten minutes only, Claire, then the children must have their tea and get ready for bed."

Claire nodded. The nurse followed Madame. The door closed and Claire looked at Louis, over Marie-Claire's soft head. He calmly led Jean-Paul towards the toy cupboard which took up one whole wall at the far end of the room. They knelt down beside it and began to get out a small army of soldiers, arranging them on the floor in battle order.

Claire sat down in the low chair and rocked Marie-Claire on her lap, singing softly to her, the old French nursery rhyme of *Frère Jácques*.

Marie-Claire, it seemed, was more than content to listen, beating time with her tiny hand on Claire's shoulder, her warm body curving into a comfortable position against Claire.

Jean-Paul, it seemed, was winning his battle against Louis's soldiers. He made explosive little sounds, bowling them over one after the other. Excited, he ran to Claire, showing her the captured soldiers.

"*Ma tante, ma tante*, see! I am beating *mon parrain*!"

Claire smiled admiringly. "What handsome soldiers! Did you have them for your birthday?"

"*Pour Noël!*" he explained. "And they were a gift from *mon oncle* Louis!" adding carefully, "That is my godfather, of course!"

"He must bring them with him to Le Petit Trésor, must he not, Aunt Claire?" Louis joined them, smiling.

Jean-Paul looked at him, wide-eyed. "Le Petit Trésor? We go there? When, *mon oncle*?"

"Soon," Louis told him. "It is a holiday! We all go—myself, your Aunt Claire, your grandmother and grandfather . . . and you, of course!"

Jean-Paul seemed delighted. "Shall I ride on your pony, Oncle Louis?"

"If you are good."

Madame returned and Claire kissed the two children. Jean-Paul suffered it, wriggling, but shook hands with Louis with great seriousness.

Claire was deeply reluctant to surrender the baby's soft warmth, but she handed her over to the nurse with a smile, and Louis at once assumed possession of her elbow once more, as though determined to enforce her continued good behaviour. A little needle of indignation shot through her. Did he expect her to make a fool of herself? He was behaving like a prison warder!

Madame said goodbye to them at the door, her heavy face warmed by a smile.

"They are beautiful children," Claire said shyly. "I think Marie-Claire has her mother's features, but Jean-Paul has her eyes. He is a very intelligent boy."

Madame inclined her head. "He is more like his father than my Madeleine, as is right in a boy! Marie-Claire is the image of her mother at that age."

"She's a darling!" Claire spoke in English, involuntarily, but Madame clearly understood her, for she smiled in response.

Then Louis was folding Claire into the car, with a stern expression, and they drew away from the Villa, and Madame, standing at the door, watching them.

"So!" Louis looked ahead unsmilingly. "You have achieved one of your ambitions, and now, I suppose, you will concentrate on achieving the other. But in that you will not succeed. Madame was aware that you had the affection for Paul that your father did not show. She knew of your letters, of your kind messages to Madeleine. She accepts you, but she will never forgive your father."

Claire did not answer. She was intent on her hands, her lips folded together with determination.

That evening she wrote to her father, describing the two children in detail, and, unconsciously, mentioning Louis rather more often than she meant to do. She explained his suggestion of a visit to the Loire with the children, touched vaguely on Madame's resistance to the idea of a visit to England for the children, and finished by assuring him that she would do all she could to promote the idea.

89

She had now explored a good deal of St. Hilaire and had got to know the narrow alleys and picturesque shopping streets rather well. She decided she preferred the harbour area to the more tourist-conscious end of town. There was a gaiety about the people there, a relaxed interest in the world around them. Even the old people, sober and reserved in their working clothes, had a smile for her when they got to know her. They resented being photographed by foreign tourists, she found, feeling that they were treated as animals in a zoo, used for background material. But when Claire investigated the cool interior of their little church, her pale hair hidden under a black scarf, and, finding a Mass in progress, stayed to kneel and watch, they greeted her outside with friendliness.

She discovered that they resented the tourist who comes into a church and talks throughout a service, wandering about disturbing the worshippers. The fact that she was eager to speak French had some influence, perhaps. They listened patiently as she sought for the right word, nodded comprehension as she waved her hands, having failed to find it, and gently suggested a suitable phrase.

The days fell into a pleasant routine. She drove out to the Villa in the morning, played or walked with the two children until lunch, which she took with Madame in the spacious dining-room. The children ate lunch upstairs and afterwards took a siesta for an hour. Claire then returned to St. Hilaire, occupied herself during the afternoon by talking to people or finding out more about the town, and returned to the hotel to change for dinner. Once or twice she dined with Louis, another evening with Pierre, who spent the whole time talking eagerly of his son Léon, who was coming to St. Hilaire for the carnival and must meet Claire.

"I have not mentioned my dream to Louis," Pierre whispered, "He finds Léon irritating. But I am sure that Léon is settling down now. He will marry and raise a family and become a good family man. I live for the day I hold my grandchildren in my arms!"

Claire felt, uncomfortably, that his glance held some hope and significance as it rested on her. If he was including her in his dream he must be disabused, but how could she rid his mind of such a fantastic notion without appearing vain? For all she knew, he might well be thinking of some other possible daughter-in-law. She might be imagining that gleam in his eye.

"You will permit Léon to take you to the carnival?" he asked eagerly. "I have not told Léon anything about you. I do not want to rush matters."

"*Monsieur*—" she began uncomfortably, but he was rising, his gaze on the dining-room behind her.

"Ah, there is Louis! And Mademoiselle Brisseut with him!" He bowed towards them. Claire half turned in her chair, her heart twisting inside her.

Louis was coming towards them, very tall and handsome in his dark lounge suit, his hand in that familiar gesture supporting the arm of the black-haired Frenchwoman whom Claire had now seen three times.

Louis looked down at Claire smilingly. "So, you dine with Pierre! I hope he entertains you!" Then he turned to his companion. "Marise, my dear, may I present Miss Claire Stratton, our young friend from

England, of whom you have heard so much. I have wished to effect this introduction for a long time."

Claire rose, her cheeks pale, and forced a smile, offering her hand.

So this was Marise? She should have guessed! But Tony's description had been misleading. From the way he spoke, she had supposed Marise to be a young girl, rather plain perhaps, since he had said she was not pretty.

Today Marise Brisseut was stunningly elegant in coffee-coloured lace, the full skirts falling to the floor, her arms and shoulders bared and gleaming in the soft light.

Claire felt dull beside her. She had put on her black dress again, having so few items from which to choose, and was aware that she looked childish beside Marise Brisseut's superb display.

It no longer surprised her that Tony should have been completely overwhelmed by Marise's personality. What had he said—that she was clever? Claire could believe it. The slanting black eyes glittered with cold intelligence. Marise was a polished mirror which reflected nothing but herself. As Claire smiled and murmured a few polite remarks, Marise watched her as if looking straight through her contemptuously, her chiselled features icily reserved. Claire, it was apparent, bored her.

She turned towards Louis, laying one white hand on his sleeve, her red mouth parting in a smile. "I have already heard of Miss Stratton from someone else, *mon cher*."

Louis shot Claire a narowed glance. "Indeed?"

Claire felt something bitter rising in her throat. She had no anticipation of what Marise was about to say, yet she knew, instinctively, that she would not like it.

"My English tutor talks of nothing else! It seems he has met her several times in the town, and I suspect he has discovered a yearning for blonde hair in the moonlight!" She laughed, showing even white teeth, her expression a little malicious as she let her dark eyes move to Claire's transfixed face.

Why was she lying? Claire was completely bewildered, shocked and incredulous as she stood there, her eyes on Marise's beautiful face.

Louis was watching her, a cruel, alien cast to his lean face. "What a pity, then, that he will so soon be leaving St. Hilaire. Their acquaintance will have to end!"

Marise gave him a gently chiding look. "Ah, Louis, you do not again threaten to have poor Monsieur Kirk expelled from town! I thought you had agreed to let him stay here."

He shrugged, his eyes cold. "He has decided to leave of his own accord. I have given him introductions to various friends of mine. He will be travelling around France, visiting famous houses, for at least six months, I imagine. He will have no time for dalliance!"

He was not looking at her now, yet Claire knew that the sharp intonation in the last words was meant for her ears.

She lowered her head and stared at the table. Pierre, a little puzzled by something he could feel in the atmosphere, looked from one to the other of them with uncertainty. He knew Louis, and he could not

93

fail to catch the ring of cruelty in his voice, yet he was unable to understand why his friend should now be looking at Claire's pale, downcast face with narrowed eyes and tightened lips. What was happening here? he asked himself.

Marise had stood very still for a moment or two, her eyes on the windows through which she could see the mild night sky, star-pitted and streaked with silver where the moon's track fell across the heavens. Her expression was unreadable, her black eyes wide and empty.

Then she turned to Louis, smiling brightly. "Are we to dine tonight, then, *mon cher*? I confess I am hungry!"

Louis automatically responded with gallantry, bidding Claire and Pierre a cool goodnight, offering Marise his arm.

Soon afterwards Claire managed to escape from Pierre by pleading a headache, and wandered out into the night to find some peace down by the whispering sea. Sand filled her shoes and slowed her progress, but she slipped the shoes off, and walked on along the wide, empty beach. The moon lay in silvery swathes over the sea, moving with the swell of the waters. Far out somewhere a ship gave a long-drawn moan, like that of a soul in torment, the sound muffled by the mist in which the ship lay hidden. Staring out to sea, Claire saw the mist rolling, low down on the water, pierced now and then by the bright spears of the moon. The wind was driving it on out to the Atlantic.

She walked aimlessly, thinking in spasms of painful intensity. Marise had lied to Louis. Why? In order to throw him off the scent, disguise her real feelings towards Tony?

Or was it to Tony that Marise had lied? Was she merely amusing herself with him while really intending to marry Louis, after all?

Claire could not decide which seemed the most plausible. She would never understand someone like Marise. They were as different as chalk and cheese. Marise wore her sophistication like armour. Tony had said that she was clever!

She stopped in her tracks, gazing around her almost with confusion. What did it matter to her, anyway? She had come out here to St. Hilaire in order to fulfil a mission for her father. Why had she allowed herself to become involved in the tangled lives of these people who were so foreign to her?

She had a sudden yearning for home, for the stark honesties of life in Trevillion. She had had no troubled thoughts there. If, at times, she had paused in her daily routine to gaze with vague longing at the horizon, wondering if she would ever know anything else but her life there, those moments had been brief and soon forgotten. She had been largely content, had even thought that she could be happy never to leave the grey rocks and seagull-haunted coves of her native country.

She needed them now. These beautiful, strange, disturbing mountains behind the town could not comfort her as could Trevillion.

Why, she asked herself, should she need comfort? What was wrong with her? She had never felt so volatile, her emotions so near the surface. Everything seemed too startlingly sharp on her sight. The moon was too bright, the shadows too dark, the air too warm and sweet. She was restless, uneasy, troubled.

Swinging suddenly, she walked back towards the hotel following the line of her own footsteps, her shoes swinging in her hands. She must hold on to her own identity, remember why she was here, and what she had to do. A strange fear kept rising into her mind, a nightmare dread of losing control of her feelings, of being plunged into a situation she did not understand.

She returned to her suite, grimly determined, and slept deeply, exhausted by some unrecognised internal battle.

Next day when Claire went out to visit the children, she asked to see Madame Treboul privately. Madame, her dark gaze bland, agreed, and ordered coffee to be sent in to them by the sallow, middle-aged maid who ran the house for her. Then, waving Claire to a seat, she asked, not unkindly, what she could do for her.

"Madame, I want you to allow me to take the children to England with me," Claire said bravely, meeting the dark eyes.

Madame's smile had disappeared. "That is out of the question," she said flatly. "I thought you understood that."

"I only want to take them there for a few days," Claire said quickly. "I would give you my word that they would be back here within a week, if you like!"

"They are too young for such a journey!" Madame leaned back, hands folded in her lap, her rings glittering in the bright sunshine.

Claire took a deep breath. "My father has been very ill, *madame*. He bitterly regrets his past attitude, and wishes to make amends. He longs to see the children, to hold them in his arms. They are his grandchildren, too, you know! Surely you can sympathise with his feelings?"

"When he has recovered," Madame said slowly, "he may visit us here and see the children. That much I will promise. But I could not permit you to remove the children from my protection." She looked at Claire gently. "It is not that I do not trust you, my dear Claire. I have learnt to have affection for you. But your father has shown himself to be hard, unrelenting and without natural affections. I could not send the children to him with a clear mind."

"Please, *madame*," Claire began, desperately ... but she was silenced.

"No more, Claire. I will not change my mind! Nothing will make me move from this decision. The children stay with me, here, and while I live they do not go to England." She looked round as the maid came in with the coffee. "Ah, here you are! Now, Claire, we shall have our coffee together and speak no more of this!"

Claire leapt up and walked to the window. "If you are quite determined, there's nothing I can say," she said in a choked voice. "I must go home to England very soon. My father will need me now."

Madame sighed. "I would prefer it if you stayed a while. The children have grown very fond of you. They need young faces around them, and I think they see in you something of their father. Certainly, Jean-

Paul has remarked several times that you are like his papa. Louis has arranged this visit to Le Petit Trésor for us. You will not want to miss that, Claire."

Didn't she? Claire thought bitterly that that was just what she did want to do. She could not bear the prospect of being in the company of Louis and Marise for very long. Marise's deceit sickened her. She felt uneasy in her presence.

Madame watched her, frowning. "I ask this of you, Claire, because of your love for the children. They need you."

"So does my father," Claire said, then bit her lip. Once before she had put her father before everything else, and lived to regret it bitterly. She had, she thought, failed Paul. She must not fail his children.

She turned and smiled faintly at Madame. "But I will come, because, as you say, the children come first."

Madame relaxed, her eyes approving. "Good. I am glad we agree on that! Come, drink your coffee. Then we shall go up and play bears with the children." Her eyes twinkled. "This is a very violent game you have taught them. Last night, Jean-Paul was growling so fiercely in his bed that I was quite alarmed."

Claire laughed. "They have so much energy! It's good for them to use it up."

Madame nodded. "That is very true. I have been concerned over this before you came. Their nurse is a sensible girl, but she does not play with them enough, and young things need play."

They drank their coffee and went up to the nursery, to be greeted ecstatically by the two little ones, and immediately dragged into a game of bears. Claire sat on the rug beside the covered fire. Jean-Paul, growling fiercely, advanced upon her from one side of the room while Marie-Claire crawled from the other. They pounced upon her, growling with deafening effect, and tickled her, breaking into joyful laughter as she pretended to be very frightened.

Claire returned to the hotel rather later than usual, since Monsieur Treboul had taken his car to be serviced and it was returned later than he had expected. He drove her back to the hotel an hour before dinner and she ran into the hotel, flushed from the drive.

Pierre stood in the reception hall, his arm around the shoulders of a slender young man, beaming upon him fondly.

Claire halted, and Pierre gave a cry of delight. "Ah, there you are, my dear! I had been hoping to see you." He gestured to his companion. "My son Léon has just arrived for the carnival! Léon, this is Claire Stratton, Paul Stratton's sister." Then he stepped back, his eyes hopeful and shining, to watch their greeting.

Claire was horribly embarrassed. She blushed hotly, holding out her hand, unable to meet the young man's eyes.

He held her hand, staring at her, and said gallantly, "This is delightful! My father did not tell me we had such a charming guest in the hotel!"

Claire glanced up and took in a faint impression of the olive skin, dark hair, dark eyes which she had expected Pierre's son to possess. What she had not expected was the incredible good looks. Léon was almost too handsome, his features feminine in their structure;

his eyes liquidly melting, his mouth perfectly shaped, his nose straight and elegant. His black hair was curly, quite short and wiry in texture, his skin as smooth as her own.

They stood there, hands entwined, staring at each other. Pierre was rapturous. He looked around, proudly expecting everyone who saw them to feel as he did, that these two were perfectly matched, the slight dark young man, the slender blonde girl. They complemented each other exactly.

One observer did not look quite as admiring as Pierre might hope. He was watching from the rear of the hall, his hands thrust into his pockets, a fixed expression on his dark face.

Pierre looked alarmed, then, glancing at his son and Claire, he shrugged. Louis might disapprove of Léon, but even he must see that if Léon had a steadying influence in his life, a girl of heart and common sense, he would soon settle down. Then . . . Pierre sighed rapturously . . . then perhaps grandchildren? A family for him to visit with many gifts, a warm, loving home for him to be part of once more! It was what he had dreamt of for so long, and Pierre was determined that somehow he would achieve his dream.

CHAPTER SIX

LÉON Frautbois was a gay, lively companion, eager to enjoy life to the full after his unbroken labours in the vineyards at Le Petit Trésor. He was far from unwilling to follow his father's advice and make friends with Claire, indeed as soon as he saw the way his father's mind was working, he determined to please him by falling into line. Léon was fond of his only parent, despite the idleness of his early years, and knew how much hurt he had inflicted by not being exactly what Pierre desired in a son. He felt only that it was fortunate that Pierre had picked out a girl with hair like spun silk and eyes like violets. Léon's filial devotion would not have been proof against a girl of lesser attractions.

St. Hilaire blossomed into gaiety on the day following Léon's sudden arrival. Flags and streamers appeared outside houses, tubs of flowers decked the streets, there were twice the usual number of foreign visitors and the local people seemed to be in a mood of relaxed anticipation. After all, their bright eyes seemed to say, it was carnival time! It came only once in a year, and why not enjoy it!

"There will be the procession in the afternoon," Léon told her. "And when it is dark, the dancing begins!"

"Dancing?"

"Through the streets," he nodded. "Everyone joins in—there are tables outside all the cafés, and singing, and the bands play until midnight. Or even later, if all is still in full swing!"

Pierre, who was having lunch with them in the hotel, looked from one to the other with a bland pleasure. He was overjoyed to see that Léon admired the fair English girl. His little plan was going smoothly.

"You are going to the carnival, Claire?" he asked with a desire to be discreet, yet blazingly obvious to both the others.

Léon winked across the table at Claire. "She must go, Papa! I shall be honoured to accompany her. A young girl could not go to the carnival alone. It might be dangerous. Sometimes the revellers become over-excited."

Claire was torn between embarrassment and amusement. She looked hesitantly at Léon. Should she refuse? He was being pushed into taking her. Perhaps there was someone else with whom he would rather go?

He read her thoughts and smiled reassurance, the thick black lashes curling down on to his smooth cheek. "Please me by agreeing to this, Claire," he added softly.

She assented then, amused by the godlike nature of his beauty, the feminine curve of cheek and mouth which aroused in her nothing but a half-protective visual pleasure. Léon had none of Louis's slightly cruel, iron strength. He was still a boy, mentally and physically. Claire wondered if he would ever grow up.

Pierre beamed, sighing with satisfaction, and said

that he must leave them. He had work to do. But they must not hurry themselves. They had all day before them. Then he departed, half envying them their youth and the enjoyment before them.

Léon met Claire's eyes and shrugged. "I am sorry that my papa has embarrassed you. He is too blatant, yes? But he has excellent taste. I would have found you myself had he not brought you to my attention."

There was a trace of conceit in his clear voice, but he was sufficiently childlike for Claire to feel no resentment.

She smiled at him, thinking that he was more like his father than she had supposed.

"I must say, I wish Monsieur Frautbois was less eager," she admitted gently.

He gave her a gay nod. "I saw your thoughts? My father has said something to you about his desire to see me settled in life?"

She agreed that he had.

Léon shrugged. "He has an obsession that I must marry and produce for him some grandchildren. It is sad, this desire to see oneself again in one's grandchildren. I have told him frankly that he should marry again and have more children. Then he would not be so unhappy over me."

"What does he say to that?"

"Oh, that he is too old!" Léon grimaced. "I do not think so, do you? He could still find a sensible woman of mature years, not incapable of bearing a child, and eager for a home of her own. I feel sometimes that he is too . . . how do you say it?"

"Possessive?" Claire hazarded.

Léon nodded. "Exactly! So, I beg you, do not concern yourself with my father. I take you to the carnival for my own sake, not for his. Does that put your mind at rest?"

She laughed. "A little. I'd better go up and change, then. I bought a suitable carnival costume this morning."

Léon rose and bowed her to the lift. Claire was amused by his transparent self-satisfaction. He really was very like his father! Although he did not look round, she could feel that he thoroughly enjoyed the little gasps of surprise and admiration which followed him as he walked out of the dining-room. He gazed down at her, smiling, yet constantly aware that his incredible good looks were arousing universal interest among the women in the hotel.

Overnight, the hotel had become quite crowded. Many people were there just for the carnival, Pierre had explained, but it meant that they were more than ordinarily busy. There had been no sign of Louis all morning. Presumably, Claire thought, he was in his office, coping with the heavier load of work.

She changed quickly into her new clothes and inspected herself in the mirror with some amusement. She had seen the skirt and blouse in a little shop that morning, and on impulse gone in to buy them. They were intended for the local girls, and were very inexpensive. The skirt was full and swirled prettily when she moved, the cotton skirts printed with a vivid design in red and black on a white background. Birds and flowers were entwined within a curling pattern of vine leaves, and the waistband was broad and emphasised the slenderness of her waist. The blouse was a white lacy cotton, very thin and delicate, worn off the shoulders, with pretty puff sleeves through the cuff of which was woven a bright red ribbon, tied with a bow at the side.

She studied her reflection, smiling. She looked very different from the prim little English girl who had arrived here. Her skin had ripened to a soft gold, pale and gleaming beside the heavy tan which a brunette could achieve, but Claire was very pleased with the way her skin had taken to the sun. She had often had to avoid the heat of the sun in England because she suffered from sunburn rather easily. Here in St. Hilaire she had taken a siesta every afternoon during the hottest part of the day, but slowly she had acquired this gentle tan.

Her shoulders, rising out of their creamy lace, had a new golden smoothness. Her silky silvery-fair hair glistened against her cheeks. Even her hair seemed to have grown more fair as sun and sea worked their spell, and her eyes shone darker than ever out of the mask of her face, their blue more vivid and more striking.

She picked up her stole and went out, smiling. As she walked towards the lift, humming to herself and dancing a little in anticipation of the fun ahead, she froze in her tracks, recognising the man who had just stepped out of the lift.

He, in turn, seemed dumbfounded by her appearance. He stared, the broad shoulders stiff, the long mouth tight below eyes that stabbed angrily.

"You have become a peasant girl for our fiesta, it

seems," he said at last, in a voice that drained the gay colour from her cheeks.

"Léon is taking me to the Carnival," Claire said weakly, suddenly frightened by the expression on his lean features. What had she done now, to make him gaze at her with that hard, glittering look? Ever since she arrived, she had been offending some one or other of his outdated codes. She no longer seemed able to guess what motivated him at all.

"Like that?" The tone whipped across her face and she flinched.

"Why not?" Her blue eyes, bewildered yet still as bright as sapphires in the small golden face, gazed back at him.

He took her arm and hustled her back towards her suite, opening the door with his own pass-key and pushing her inside with a hand that bruised her bare skin.

In a moment she was in her bedroom, facing her mirror, and he stood at her back, his grey eyes biting into hers in their dual mirrored reflection.

"Look at yourself! You look like some little fisher-girl getting ready to go out with her boy! These people all know you are staying here in my hotel, as my personal guest. What will they think when they see you like this?"

Defiance came to her with a gust of anger. "What will they think? Probably that I'm enjoying their carnival with a handsome young man! And why should I not? What else is the carnival for? All the other girls will be wearing clothes like this, and dancing with their young men. I see nothing wrong in that!"

He had an electric glitter in his eyes now, the broad shoulders very close to her own, his long thin hands gripping her shoulders, the thumbs moving over her smooth skin.

"So! You are breaking out of that cocoon of English sobriety at last! And you choose to amuse yourself with another of these weaklings. First Kirk, now Léon, who is a French version of the same thing. I ask myself why it is that you prefer these men, and I can only decide that you are afraid!"

"Afraid?" Claire heard herself echo the word, and felt the violent leaping of her heart at the same time. The continual movement of those strong fingers against her shoulders was creating in her a smouldering hunger which frightened her, in truth.

"Of anything more demanding!" He swung her round to face him, his eyes leaping over her, touching on the smooth, hollowed shoulders rising out of the lace, the pulse beating in her slender throat, the quiver at the pink mouth.

"You . . . you're hurting me. . . ." she said faintly, putting up her own hands to push him away.

He laughed, his lips curling back. "You should not dress in this . . ." he flipped a contemptuous finger at her blouse, "if you do not expect to excite attention." His hands travelled down her arms to her wrists, seized them in a savage grip, and held her prisoner, glaring down at her.

"Why do you think this blouse leaves the shoulders bare?" he demanded. "To intrigue and excite the men you will dance with, to make them long to touch that smooth skin of yours with their hands, or their lips. . . ." He slowly lowered his head until his mouth rested on the curve of her naked shoulder.

Claire felt a fierce, trembling pleasure at the light pressure, and her breath was drawn inwards harshly. His mouth moved up towards her neck, lingering hotly where her pulse beat, betraying her fear and emotion.

Instinct made her want to touch his hair, stroke the bent dark head which was so close, but she only struggled to break the grip on her wrists.

"Let me go . . . this is. . . ." The words panted out wildly, and he raised his head to look into her eyes.

"Did you imagine that you could arouse men's interest and yet escape untouched?" he asked mockingly. "The very fact that you choose to wear this costume is like a green light to them! I am only showing you what to expect if you go out into the streets at night like this!"

"All the men of St. Hilaire will not be savages," she flung at him, and was half pleased, half sorry, to see the dark face flinch.

But he was smiling again in the next moment, an ironic, wounding smile. "In that costume you will arouse the savage hidden in every man. Yes, even in Léon, who is weak and silly enough normally! Now, you will change into something more English. I will wait outside."

"I will not change!" Claire knew, as she flung the challenge, that she was risking another angry exchange with him, but her independence could not be forced down. It was ridiculous for him to browbeat and bully her like this. In England her costume would pass unnoticed. Bare shoulders and arms were demure compared to the bikini-clad girls she had seen on the beach at St. Hilaire only this morning. Because she was not an ordinary tourist there was no reason why Louis should feel free to dictate to her, as though she were a convent-bred little schoolgirl.

He stared at her, nostrils flaring. "You will do as I say!"

Silently she shook her head, holding his eyes defiantly.

For a long moment he was still. She nerved herself for a further outbreak of violence. It hung in the air between them, hot and pulsing, filling her veins with electric warning. Then he swung on his heel and left, slamming the door behind him.

Claire collapsed into a chair, trembling. Fatally she knew that he would never forgive her for that act of defiance. Louis's stern code admitted no defeat, and he would not forget that she had won this engagement.

She closed her eyes tightly, reliving the moment when his mouth had burned against her throat. A bitter taste filled her mouth. She buried her face in her hands, admitting what she had refused to consider until now.

She was in love with Louis de Carceron.

It had happened at their first moment of meeting. One glance from those grey eyes and she had felt a pang of foreboding. She had kept her growing feeling for him locked away in her heart because she knew the complete folly of it.

It was insanity to imagine that he would look at

her, except in cold criticism. He regarded her as he would any young girl put into his care. He thought of her only as Paul's little sister, a rather wilful child, to be punished when she transgressed. Even the kisses which had forced her to admit her hungry yearnings for him had been a punishment, a warning. His experience of other, more beautiful women had taught him how to kiss and punish at the same time. He could not, must not, ever guess that those brief moments had awoken in her a desire for more of his kisses.

Hot blood swept up over her shoulders, throat and face as she thought of the humiliation she would undergo if he ever guessed. Rather than see scorn and pity in those grey eyes she would die!

It was ten minutes before she felt able to go downstairs to face Léon. She wrapped her stole around her shoulders, shivering a little, as she greeted him.

He was reproachful. "I thought you had changed your mind, Claire, and were going to abandon me!" Then his liquid eyes ran over her and he smiled. "But how beautiful you look! It suits you, that costume. I shall be the envy of St. Hilaire! We shall dance until the stars go down into the sea and all the little fishes come out to stare in amazement!"

She laughed, her mood becoming hectically gay. "First we must watch the procession, Léon! Where is the best place to stand?"

"Beside the market square," he said, taking her hand. "Come, we must hurry, or we shall miss the best floats!"

They pushed their way into the throng which stood

three deep beside the market square just as the first float passed. Claire gasped at the brilliance of the flowers which formed the name St. Hilaire, surrounded by a design of blue sea, silver fishes and golden suns. Thousands of flowers had been used to make the float —carnations, rhododendrons, mistinguette, tiny white daisies, packed tightly together and expertly trimmed to present a smooth surface.

Then a band marched past, instruments blaring, their shakoes nodding under the movement of their owners. Blue and white uniforms, carefully pressed, with silver buttons shining, the band marched with proud self-importance. The crowd applauded them, some calling out names of boy-friends or relatives. The young men looked sideways, grinning, perspiration glistening on their foreheads.

Other floats appeared. Castles of camellias with beautiful local girls leaning out of their battlements; boats with sails of roses; a dragon with vicious red eyes made of crimson petals, on whose flowery back rode a small, laughing band of children with flowers in their hair.

The crowd clapped and called out, laughed, pointed, enthused loudly at each new beauty.

Léon looked down at Claire, his liquid eyes dancing. "It is fun, no?"

"Yes!" she laughed back, determined to extract the last ounce of enjoyment from the day which she had insisted upon at such cost.

When the procession of floats was over, the last echo of the bands vanishing into the distance, the crowd began to drift away into the side streets and alleys. Léon took Claire's hand and led her back to the little café at which she had met Tony Kirk, telling her happily that they would take a coffee together while waiting for the hour of dinner.

"We dine at the hotel, of course, then come back to St. Hilaire for the dancing."

The café was already crowded with gay customers. A boy in a blue silk shirt was strumming on a guitar, singing softly to his companions. The waiter was darting about hastily, serving coffees and glasses of cool drinks. At a far table sat Tony Kirk, a glass in front of him, a look of weariness on his fair face.

Claire murmured to Léon, who looked curious but said nothing, "I see a friend. Will you excuse me for a moment?"

She paused beside Tony's table and he looked up eagerly, only to have the light fade from his eyes as he recognised her.

"Oh, hallo, Claire! How are you? I rang you at the hotel a couple of times, but they always said you weren't available." He gestured to the free chair beside him. "Will you have a drink?"

"No, thank you. I'm with someone."

"Louis?" he asked bitterly, his mouth turning down at the corners.

Claire shook her head. "No. He did speak to you, didn't he? I gave him the list and he said he would do what he could for you."

Tony shrugged. "Yes, he gave me some letters of introduction. He paid my debts, too. I'm to pay him back when I get the money."

"That was kind of him!" She spoke with forced

enthusiasm, but she could see that something was very wrong from Tony's drooping shoulders.

Tony's mouth twitched. "Oh, sure! He could afford to pay to get rid of me! He was going to get what he wanted, after all." He looked at her with wounded eyes. "Marise is going to marry him after all. Did you know? Ironic, isn't it? My hope of being able to marry her depended on the one man determined to see that I never should. He must have laughed when you asked him to help me leave St. Hilaire. He knew by then that Marise had decided to obey her parents and marry him."

Claire stood very still, willing herself to stay calm. So Louis was going to marry Marise! Well, she had expected it.

"Are you certain?" She watched him and knew that only a dull conviction of total disaster could make the carefree, light-minded Tony look as miserable as this.

He shrugged. "She told me so herself. She has decided that I would never be able to give her the sort of life she needs, the money to buy her sort of clothes, enjoy her sort of pleasures. So I've been given my ticket and told to blow!"

Pity racked her. She bent over him, touching his shoulder. "Don't take it so hard, Tony. She isn't worth all this!"

"Isn't she?" He looked up, trying to smile, but only managing to look like the ruins of his former self. "Maybe I'll tell myself that in a year from now. For the moment I'm wondering how to start picking up the pieces. I was always a footloose sort of chap, Claire.

I have never been this deeply involved before, but she really got under my skin."

"Where's your pride?" she chided gently. "You don't want to give her the satisfaction of knowing she's done this to you, do you?"

He laughed wryly. "Oh, she knows! She knows only too well. There's a cruel streak in her, just as there is in Louis. She even accused me of having flirted with you. Obviously, that was just an excuse. She knows I'm too mad about her to look at another girl." He sat upright, pulling himself together. "But thanks for trying to help me, Claire. It was good of you. I only wish I had better news to tell you."

She smiled brightly. "What will you do now? Go back home?"

"No, I think I'll use Louis's introductions. I might as well get something out of this mess. I'll write my book, then I'll go home and try for that job." He stood up. "Goodbye, Claire. Nice to have known you." He kissed her cheek lightly. "Don't make my mistake, will you? Love is the very devil!"

Claire watched him walk away, feeling sad and angry and very troubled. His warning came too late for her. She had to face the same heartbreak, watch Louis marrying another girl, but she was fiercely determined never to betray herself by so much as a flicker.

She rejoined Léon and received a look of curious reproach. "How did you meet Tony Kirk? Did you know him in England? I would have joined you, but your conversation seemed very private."

She smiled. "Tony isn't feeling very happy at the

moment. He's leaving St. Hilaire tomorrow, I gather."

Léon nodded. "Louis has always wanted him to go. I am not surprised to hear the news. He is pleasant, but he did not pay his bills, and that makes Louis very angry."

"What has it got to do with Louis?" she asked angrily.

Léon looked surprised. "Many of the shops are owned by Louis and rented to local people. He is very wealthy. That is no doubt why the Brisseut family are eager for an alliance. You have met Raoul Brisseut? He is not so wealthy as Louis, but he is ambitious. He has long desired to see his daughter married to Louis. Once he hoped she would make a match in Paris, where she was studying fashion design, but it fell through, and she came home last year for good. She is no longer so young, and she is looking for a suitable husband. I expect the marriage will be announced soon."

Claire nodded. She was tired of the subject. It merely depressed her.

Léon was grinning now, though. "Marise Brisseut will have no easy time with Louis, though. He is as tough as leather, and totally ruthless Marise will meet her match."

Good for Marise, Claire thought cynically. She'll have a husband to be proud of! A ruthless, cruel man without any of the gentler emotions.

Why had she chosen to fall in love with such a man? She must be out of her mind! I will not let myself love him, she thought fiercely. I'll push him out of my mind somehow.

Léon was looking at her in surprise and she realised he had been speaking to her.

"I'm sorry?"

"I asked if you were ready to return to the hotel for dinner?" he asked again.

"Yes, of course," she said lightly.

They dined by candlelight in the private, management alcove, to the soft whisper of violin strings and the magic gaiety of coloured lanterns outside in the dark garden, shining like strange fruits in the trees. Léon was charmingly attentive, paying her elaborate compliments, his dark eyes constantly moving over her with ardent admiration.

Someone, presumably Pierre, had arranged a vase of pure white camellias on the table, and Léon picked one out and gently threaded the stem through Claire's silvery hair.

They returned to the town and danced in the crowds which filled the narrow streets. Overhead shone the coloured lanterns, lifting in the warm night air, shedding gay chequered patterns of colour on the upturned faces of the people.

Léon held Claire's waist firmly, her hand entwined with his, and whispered his flowery compliments now and then as they danced. She wondered how it was possible that in such a situation she should be so miserable. Here she was, dancing through picturesque streets in a little French town, under magic lanterns of blue and red and yellow, while the most handsome young man she had ever seen paid her extravagant and unbelievable compliments, and she was not enjoying it in the slightest.

Most girls would be having the time of their lives! But she had had to ruin her holiday by falling in love with Louis de Carceron, and for that piece of folly she would have to pay.

Léon kept her dancing until the night was well advanced, and a large number of their fellow dancers had drifted away to their homes. The band still played on, faces perspiring, eyes shining, keeping time with their feet, but there were fewer and fewer people to dance to the lilting music, and the street cafés were now almost empty.

At last Claire begged Léon to take her back to the hotel, and with easy good nature he agreed, regretting that the evening should so soon be over.

Léon appeared to have enjoyed himself. He hummed all the way back to the hotel, holding Claire's hand and swinging it.

Overhead the deep purple sky was pierced with stars of cold brilliance. The sound of the sea murmured in her ears continually and the warm air was like wine to her tired lungs.

When they walked into the reception hall she felt every nerve in her body jolt as though with an electric shock. Louis was standing, talking to Pierre and Marise Brisseut, his back half turned towards the entrance.

Pierre saw the newcomers and exclaimed eagerly. Léon grinned at him, still holding Claire's hand. She might have pulled her hand free had she not been intent on hiding from Louis de Carceron that she felt anything for him but dislike. As it was, she let Léon slide his arm around her waist as they joined the other little group, and she smiled brightly at Pierre, who looked almost dazzled with joy.

"You have enjoyed yourselves, *mes enfants*?" he asked, his voice deep with emotion.

Léon sighed dramatically, his eloquent glance answer enough.

Pierre patted his son's cheek. "That is very good! Ah, to be young and enjoy the carnival with a beautiful young girl!" He beamed at Claire. "You have stars in your eyes tonight, my dear Claire!"

Did she? They must be stars of wounded pride, of hopelessness, of defiance. She smiled back at him, willing herself to look as though she were the happiest girl in the world. But she could not force herself to speak, for fear of a betraying quiver in her voice.

Marise was studying her with unconcealed distaste. "You went to the carnival like that?" One fine dark brow lifted in disbelief. "It was not wise. Fortunate for you that Léon was with you!"

Léon looked down at Claire. Their eyes met and he frowned, seeing for the first time the pain in her wide dark blue eyes. Quickly, on a generous impulse, he said, "Claire looks enchanting in her gay costume. She has been much admired tonight, and I much envied. At a carnival, we all like to do mad things!"

Claire was grateful, and smiled at him. At her side, in a voice as cold as winter snow, Louis said, "Nevertheless, she will not again wear this peasant costume. Tomorrow it will be consigned to the flames, where it belongs."

Pierre looked anxious and perturbed. "Why, Louis,

you cannot be serious! Poor Claire will think you disapprove of her pretty costume!"

Driven by pain and despair into an act of further defiance, Claire looked at Louis, seeing his austerely handsome features with a steely determination not to be moved by them. "I know he disapproves of it," she said lightly, her mouth moving into a hard bright smile. "I'm afraid I don't care whether he does or not! I shall keep the costume always, as a memento of a very delightful evening." Then she turned, stood on her toes to kiss Léon on his startled mouth, and fled into the lift.

CHAPTER SEVEN

IT was heartrending to awake next morning into the sun-bright world of St. Hilaire, to open one's eyes to the dazzle of the sky and sea and hear the long romantic murmur of the waves as they caressed the shore.

Claire lay, lids shuttered down, longing for the stormy desolation of Trevillion. At least there one knew that the violence was all outside, raging with the elements, while inside the square, self-confident little house one could be warm and safe. Here in St. Hilaire she had found the opposite. Gaiety and beauty outside, while storms raged within.

She drew in a long, painful breath and swung out of bed. She must face the day some time—the sooner the better.

She came down into the reception hall, hoping to see no one, but Pierre was there, hovering with an expression of bruised hope and resignation. He hurried towards her, almost wringing his hands as he came.

"Claire, I have sad news for you. Léon has returned to Le Petit Trésor . . . he is desolated that he could not see you before he left. He left with me his grateful thanks and his hope that he would see you again soon. . . ." But she could see from Pierre's downcast eyes that he merely used a formula. Had Léon taken fright at his papa's urgent desire to marry him off?

She smiled at the older man, comforting him. "What a pity! Never mind, it was fun last night. I shall always remember my first carnival with much pleasure."

Pierre glanced behind him, almost with furtive eyes, then said softly, "I could see that Léon also enjoyed it. When you are at Le Petit Trésor, you will be able to see him again. I hope you will wish to do so, Claire. Léon is not so black as Louis would paint him! He has fine instincts at times. Last night I was proud of him."

Claire stiffened. Louis? What did Pierre mean? "Last night, Pierre?" she queried quickly. "What happened last night?"

Pierre glanced around again with the same furtive look. "Louis was very angry. He sent Léon back to Le Petit Trésor, and ordered him to leave at first light. I was alarmed by the coldness of Louis's manner. He has never understood Léon, but last night I felt . . ." he frowned uneasily, "I felt almost that he hated him! Louis has very strict ideas, you will have seen. He has a strong sense of family, and to him you are almost like a sister, since Paul was his dear friend. He fears, I think, that Léon would hurt you. Me, I told him Léon would not do so. And Léon himself was very frank about his admiration and respect for you." He sighed. "It was good to hear the boy speak so well. But Louis was unconvinced."

"So he dismissed Léon as though he was a servant?" Claire was incredulous. How could anyone behave with such autocratic cruelty and get away with it? Léon was not a boy. He could have refused!

But when she said as much, Pierre seemed taken

aback. "Léon could not disobey Louis, Claire. You must not despise him for accepting Louis's decision. Louis employs him." He shrugged. "And myself, also, of course! Louis has been very good to Léon and myself. We owe him more than I can tell you. It was Louis who paid for Léon's good education. When Louis built this hotel he made me manager, although I had never held so important a position before, and I can never repay the many debts I owe him." He looked anxiously at her. "You must understand, Claire, how it is with us. Léon may protest, he may even feel rebellious, but he knows that it would be ungrateful of him to disobey."

She was sorry for him. He was such a nice man and he looked so unhappy. She smiled gently and touched his hand. "I do understand, Pierre. Don't look so worried. It is natural that you should wish to please your employer."

He looked eagerly at her. "And there will be other occasions, Claire! While you are at Le Petit Trésor. . . . You will not let this influence you against Léon? I am convinced that it was the lack of a mother's care that has made my boy so restless, never settling down or finding anything he really cares for in life. A father cannot give his son that anchor which a mother provides. When Léon finds the right wife, he will no longer be blown like a feather in every wind."

Claire laughed. "You may be right, Pierre. Now I must go. I shall be late at the Villa if I don't hurry."

As she drove through the town, she wondered how she was going to break it to Pierre that she was not interested in his son. Why were men so difficult? Her father had broken his heart over Paul's marriage, and here was Pierre trying desperately to force his son into a marriage Léon did not want. If only they could let their children live their own lives, instead of trying to live for them! Human beings were complex and strange. It was easy for an outsider to see what was wrong, yet there was no way of bringing the truth home to those directly involved, since their personal feelings blinded them to the truth.

Léon was a gay and charming young man, but he was not yet adult enough for marriage, and to try to rush him would only lead to disaster.

In that, she admitted reluctantly, Louis was right. It was not his decision so much as his way of enforcing it that galled!

He must have seen that Pierre was manipulating them into a difficult position and decided to cut the strings by sending Léon packing. The very fact that Louis had such insight and clear-headed common sense made her angry. She resented the way in which he comprehended a situation and took steps to resolve it rapidly.

Who was he to play God, anyway? It was infuriating. Why couldn't he be wrong, for once? What if he had been wrong? What if she had fallen in love with Léon? Louis's precipitate behaviour might have done irreparable harm.

Claire found the children waiting eagerly when she arrived at the Villa. They had planned to take a stroll through the narrow lanes towards a little farmhouse which boasted the delights of some goats, pigs and a litter of new puppies.

Claire had already discussed with Madame a certain plan which she meant to put into operation this morning, and now she exchanged a smiling glance with the heavy-featured older woman, asking a silent question. Madame nodded, gave an astonishing, lively wink which made Claire laugh out loud. There had been a great change in their relationship lately. Madame, missing her daughter and eager for sympathetic young company, had allowed herself to become fond of Claire, particularly as the two children loved Claire's company. Madame was not a jealous grandmother. She was prepared to love anyone who loved the children.

She was not to accompany them on their walk. It was, she said, too far for her old legs.

"Are your legs older than the rest of you, Grand'-mère?" asked Jean-Paul with serious interest.

Madame smiled and touched his head. "I sometimes think they must be, *mon petit*. Now, off you go with Tante Claire. Be good, and do just as she bids you."

Marie-Claire, strapped safely into her light push-chair, clutching a wax-featured doll with widely open eyes, kicked her legs eagerly as they set off. She was hoping to be allowed to walk for a while later, but meanwhile the fascinating vistas engrossed her attention.

Banks starred with wild flowers, gates through which she could glimpse other villas, trees leaning low over their heads, their branches thick with birds—Marie-Claire found them all enchanting.

When they reached the farmhouse they were met by a smiling woman in black, her weathered face

124

wrinkled by a thousand lines, who offered them refreshment in her sunny kitchen. Claire had met her once before, and was delighted by the cheerful, yet primitive, little house; the stone trough outside the back door where the farmer washed in icy water in the morning, the flagged floors which reminded her of Trevillion, the vast black range on which bubbled pots and kettles. She seated the two children at the scrubbed wooden table. The farmer's wife brought them freshly baked sponge cakes, *sirop* and a little plate of crystallised fruit. For Claire she had provided coffee and a slice of thickly spread chocolate cake.

Claire was placed in an old rocking chair, whose black polished surface shone like the sun, her back resting against a heap of soft cushions stuffed, the woman told her proudly, with feathers from their own ducks.

They talked for a while, sipping their coffee in a relaxed atmosphere. The sun shone through the small windows on a sill lined with potted plants whose bright flowers seemed to reach up towards the light. A marmalade cat lay on a home-made rag rug before the range. An old clock, its tarnished face almost unreadable, ticked away on the mantel.

When the children had finished, the farmer's wife took them by their hands, and led them out to a small barn. Here they found a honey-coloured labrador sleeping in a patch of sunlight, curled around a pile of tiny little bodies which snuffled as near to her as they could reach.

Jean-Paul gave a low cry and fell to his knees in the straw, his hands tentatively touching the curl of, one dog's warm body. The mother raised her head, regarded him intently, then, deciding that he was harmless, lay down again. The puppies, tumbling over each other, climbed up to lick the little boy's hands and face. Marie-Claire toddled forward, chattering to herself, and squatted down to take her share of the love the little dogs were eager to expend.

Claire watched them lovingly. Their faces shone with joy and affection. Jean-Paul, his arms full, laughed aloud. Marie-Claire gasped breathlessly as one of the puppies nipped at her fingers in an attempt to capture her attention.

She waited a moment, then said softly, "Wouldn't it be nice to take one of these puppies home with us?"

Jean-Paul turned, eyes huge, not quite believing that it could be possible. Marie-Claire was less tentative. She nodded her head eagerly.

"I want one! I want one!"

Jean-Paul considered Claire's face intently. "Grand'-mère would let us?"

Claire smiled and nodded. "You are the eldest, Jean-Paul. You may choose. But one only! And you must be very good to the little dog. You must not squeeze him too hard, or pull his tail."

Jean-Paul gazed down at the tumbling litter, at eager black noses and pink tongues. He sighed. "Which one?" he asked himself, shaking his head.

Then minutes later they returned to the Villa, Jean-Paul walking close to the push-chair in which his little sister squirmed, his eyes fixed on the small basket which Claire carried, resting on the handle of the chair.

"What shall we call him?" he demanded.

"You choose the name," Claire invited.

He frowned. "Will he grow big like his mother?"

She nodded. "And the same lovely honey colour!"

"Then we will call him that," he said firmly. "Miel."

Miel, Claire thought. Honey! "It sounds like a girl's name," she said gently.

"It is good," he said firmly. "Miel!" He touched the wicker basket, calling softly, "Miel, Miel!" And from within a husky, uncertain little yap answered him. He laughed. "See, he knows it is his name!" He looked round at Claire. "Did you have a dog when you were little, Claire?"

She smiled reminiscently. "Yes, we had a dog. Your father called him Nip because he used to bite."

"Pincer?" Jean-Paul used the French word doubtfully. "That is a good word for a dog, but I hope Miel does not bite hard."

"He seems a good-natured little animal," Claire said reassuringly.

"Tell me about when you and my papa were little," the boy invited.

She told him stories about Paul as a boy all the way back to the Villa, and he listened with fascination.

Madame was apparently very surprised to see the puppy, and pretended to be taken aback. Nervously, Jean-Paul assured her that Miel would be very good.

"I hope so," she said severely. "I shall expect you to teach him how to behave in a nice home! Take him now for a walk down to the end of the garden, Jean-Paul, and see that he does not eat my flowers!"

The nurse took Marie-Claire up to the nursery for her nap, since the long walk in the fresh air had made her sleepy, and Madame invited Claire to stay for lunch.

"I have been speaking to Louis on the telephone," she told her. "He regrets that it will be impossible for us to go to Le Petit Trésor for a week. He is too busy at the hotel."

Claire felt sure that this decision had more to do with Léon than with Louis's business. She gazed out of the window, watching Jean-Paul and the puppy rolling on the smooth lawn.

Madame's gaze followed hers, and her face relaxed into one of her warm smiles.

"The boy loves this little dog, no? You were right to suggest it, Claire. Marie-Claire is not old enough to be company for her brother, and boys need to play such energetic games. I am glad you thought of a puppy."

"Where will he sleep?"

"In the kitchen, for the moment. We have prepared a snug box for him to sleep in and he will have a little door made for him to go in and out. I only hope we do not spoil him too much."

Hesitantly, Claire said, "I really think I should go home next week, *madame*. My father will need me. I have been here several weeks now. My sister will be wanting to return to London."

Madame looked distressed. "But the children, Claire . . . they will miss you so much." She hesitated, then added, "I also will miss you. It is pleasant to have these little visits from you every day. I was going to suggest that you move into the Villa until we leave for Le Petit Trésor, but Louis thought you would prefer to be in St. Hilaire where there is so much to entertain you."

Louis again! Claire almost choked with rage. "I would have been delighted to stay with you," she said quickly. "I wish you had asked me."

Madame looked quickly at her. "Really? That is very good of you, Claire. Then you will postpone your return and come to stay here for a few days?"

"I'll gladly come to stay for a few days," Claire said, "but I really think I shouldn't put off my return home. I can't help being anxious about my father. I've had only one short letter since I got here, and that told me nothing of how matters stood at home. If I can't take the children to see him, I should go home myself."

Madame sighed. "I know you feel badly about my refusal to let you take the children, Claire, but I beg that you will try to see things from my point of view. I love these children dearly. I do not want them to go so far away, especially so soon after...."

"I understand," Claire said quickly, seeing that Madame was deeply distressed at the memory of Paul and Madeleine's deaths. "And I'll do all I can to make my father understand. As soon as he's really well, I'll persuade him to come to France with me, and see the children in their own home." She looked at Madame, her eyes pleading. "You will let him see them, won't you, *madame*? It would mean so much to him!"

Madame shrugged. "I will, Claire. I think I can forgive him in time. It will be hard, but I will try."

Claire smiled at her. "Thank you."

She promised to return to the Villa later that day, when she had collected her belongings from the hotel and made arrangements with Pierre to send on any letters which arrived.

She got back to the hotel during the silent hour of siesta, while everyone was resting in their rooms after a prolonged lunch, and made her way to her suite to pack. She was just walking round to make sure she had forgotten nothing when there was a tap on her door and Louis entered. Claire felt her senses leap at the sight of him, and a pulse began to beat at her temple, but she managed a cool smile.

"Good afternoon. I was going to leave a message with Pierre to tell you. . . ."

He broke in with icy hauteur. "I know what you meant to let Pierre tell me! I have spoken with Madame. You can unpack your things. You are not going to the Villa!"

Claire was almost too angry for speech.

She stared at him, trembling. What had he done now? The lean, handsome face was bent down towards her, the grey eyes impassively cold, the strong mouth taut. She knew that he was capable of reading every fleeting expression in her own face, and struggled to gain control of her reactions.

When she felt calm enough, she asked coolly, "I don't understand you, *monsieur*. Why am I not to go to the Villa? It's all arranged between Madame Treboul and myself."

He gestured, his broad shoulders lifting in a very

Gallic shrug. "I have cancelled the arrangement!" His tone was airy, confident and infuriating.

"What right have you to do such a thing? I don't accept anyone's right to interfere in my affairs. I shall only be here for a few days now, and I intend to spend as much time as possible with the children."

"Madame told me you plan to return home very soon," he said indifferently. "It will not be necessary, however."

"Not necessary? Why not? I explained to Madame Treboul that my father needs me and I must go."

"You are angry because I sent Léon away," he said, his mouth twisting with distaste. "I only acted for the best. It was not wise of you to permit Pierre to make these foolish dreams. Léon is not mature enough to enter into any lasting relationship. Pierre has spoiled him."

"Pierre is foolish," she admitted, "but he acted out of love for his son. I understood, and so, I assure you, did Léon. There was never any need for you to interfere." Her voice rose sharply as her anger grew, anger which was only intensified by the pain it gave her to look at him and feel the hopelessness of the emotion he aroused in her. "But you can't be satisfied, can you, unless you're meddling with other people's lives? You're convinced that you know best for everyone. Well, you do *not* know what's best for me. Only I know that, and I will not meekly submit to being manipulated!"

"You prefer being caressed by Léon?" he demanded sharply. "You enjoyed having him hold your hand? I know you kissed him merely to defy me—that was plain. But what went before? Léon did not seem totally amazed by that kiss. Had you already, perhaps, exchanged kisses in the darkened streets while you danced?"

"What if we had? What business would it be of yours?" Her cheeks were hot, her eyes fiery as she stared back at him. "It seemed to me to be expected of us. We danced among a crowd of other young people, and I saw many kisses exchanged. There was no outcry from the older people watching from the cafés. In fact, I thought they seemed quite approving. It was all part of the fun."

He was silent for a long moment, his narrowed eyes probing hers. "Are you telling me you think yourself in love with Léon?" he asked slowly.

Claire shook her head. "No, I'm not in love with him. I like him and I enjoyed his company, that's all."

"Yet you let him kiss you while you danced? I know that English girls are allowed more freedom than we think wise, but surely you do not kiss every man who dances with you?"

She had a sudden searing memory of the kiss he had forced upon her on the previous evening, the warmth of his mouth on her shoulder and throat. Her eyes fell, her mouth quivered. "No," she said faintly. "No, I do not let every man who dances with me kiss me. . . . I'm very careful whom I allow to kiss me."

"Yet you kissed Léon?"

"You said yourself that I did it to defy you," she admitted. "I can't understand your attitude. I never shall. You seem to be a hundred years out of date."

"I understand the French mind," he said calmly,

"and you do not! If you imagine that in the remote rural areas they would be as permissive as the people of Paris, you are sadly mistaken. St. Hilaire is two places. One side of the town is used to the excesses of the English tourist, shrugs its shoulders and turns the blind eye. The other side is shocked by brief skirts and too much make-up, believes the worst if it sees a young girl kissing a boy in the public street, and condemns what it does not practise. You are not a tourist—I have told you this before. You are related to the Trebouls, and your conduct reflects on them. If you are believed to be loose in conduct your family will be condemned as too lax in their control of you."

"It's archaic!" she protested.

"It is France," he returned evenly. "You forget, in some parts of France we are still old-fashioned enough to believe in morality and purity."

"You can't expect me to believe you're sincere," she flung in sudden challenge. "You proved otherwise last night. Is it moral for a man to kiss a girl forcibly in order to teach her a lesson? Are kisses permissible as a punishment but not as a pleasure?"

His lean features tightened, the grey eyes flashed. "Was that all it was, Claire? A punishment?"

The tone startled and confused her. Did he mean . . .? She could not meet his eyes. What did he mean?

After a long moment he spoke again, in a different voice, steady and calm. "I sent Léon back to Le Petit Trésor because I have decided to have him trained as a sales representative. He leaves for Paris to meet our main buyers in two days' time. It may suit him better

133

to be in the sales department. He has a persuasive tongue and a pleasant manner. Pierre will be able to visit him in Paris now and then."

"Does Pierre know all this?"

"I have not yet discussed it with him, but he will be happy when he hears about it."

"I'm sure he will," she said, a little acidly. "Pierre, it seems, is happy with whatever you suggest. Perhaps you ought to find Léon a bride, then you could all be happy."

"I have given that some thought," he admitted calmly, apparently unaware of the sarcasm in her voice. "Pierre may be right to wish to find Léon a good, sensible wife. It may steady him. I must look about for one."

"Just like that?" Claire was incredulous. "It wouldn't matter, I suppose, that Léon didn't love her, nor she him. It would be a neat, tidy arrangement for all concerned! I think you're all perfectly insane!"

Louis laughed. "I would be more subtle than Pierre," he said softly. "I would introduce the bride to Léon, let him see how charming she was and then leave it up to him. With someone like Léon, love is not a deep emotion. He is incapable of such a feeling. He would only desire a pretty, capable girl who would be prepared to be fond of him. You do not understand Léon, my dear Claire. He is one of those who float on the surface of life. He likes to be comfortable and easy. A real emotion would merely puzzle and disturb him."

"You make him sound like a puppet! A wooden doll on strings which you can pull at will."

"Claire," he began sharply, but was cut short as the telephone rang in her bedroom. She walked through to answer it, and called to him.

"It's for you."

He stood beside her bed, speaking into the receiver with crisp clipped tones. Claire moved quickly away, back into the sitting-room, but heard him say, "Marise? My dear, how are you?"

Her head burned with humiliation and misery. She went to the window and stared out, willing herself to remain calm on the outside. She would rather die than have him guess how she felt. Jealousy stung, deep inside her, like a mortal wound. What must it be like to have Louis speak to one in those soft, caressing tones he was now using? His voice had altered as he realised to whom he spoke, had grown gentle and affectionate.

He never spoke to her like that. Harsh, domineering, over-protective, like an angry father, he seemed to regard her as a difficult and naughty child to be bullied into safety. He thought of her, as he thought of Léon, as people for whom he was responsible.

She must get away from him, and soon. She picked up her case and arranged her other bags beside the door, ready to be taken down by the porter later.

Louis came back, saw what she was doing and said, "I told you, Claire, you are staying here. You are not going to the Villa."

"You gave me no good reason," she said abruptly. "And without one, I intend to go to the Villa as planned."

"I have a very good reason," he said coolly. "But I do not want to tell you about it at present. I merely ask you to do as I require. Stay here." The grey gaze fixed her eyes, held them, willing her to do as he suggested. She felt herself weakening under the impact of his charm, the smile which slid around his mouth, making his eyes warm and persuasive.

"How do I know you're not just tricking me into staying?" she asked. "If you have a reason, tell me now!"

He shrugged. "It is a little secret which I wish to keep to myself a little while. Please, Claire, do as I ask this once, without arguing!"

She shrugged. "Very well." There was a strange feeling inside her as she spoke, a sensation of relief, as though it comforted her to give in to Louis on this occasion.

He laughed, delighted. "There is no need to look as though I asked the impossible. Come, we will go for a stroll through the gardens. The heat is lessening again. We shall go as far as the beach, perhaps. You will tell me how you are getting on with Madame and the children, and all about this puppy you have persuaded Madame to buy for the children."

"I bought it," Claire explained, smiling at the memory. "I heard about the puppies from Madame Treboul, and thought that it might be good for Jean-Paul to have one. She agreed at once, and I bought it for them as my farewell present."

"You are quite content to leave them?" he asked acutely, watching her face. "It does not trouble you to say goodbye? I would have said you had a tender heart where such matters were concerned."

"I hate leaving them," she said hotly. "But I'm worried about my father."

"What would happen to your father if you married?" he asked. "You could not expect your husband to live at Trevillion. Or do you really intend to go home and marry this young farmer who lives nearby? Perhaps, for all your talk of freedom, you will marry for a practical reason in the end, and not for love!"

"I believe in crossing my bridges when I come to them," she said lightly.

They left her suite and crossed to the lift. Louis stood at her side, very tall and handsome, his hand under her elbow. Very softly, he said to her, "You are quite right to dream of love, Claire, and I am sure that you will find it, if you open your heart to life instead of building a wall around yourself. You talk of freedom, yet you have a broken look at times, as though you were walled up in an ice palace. Fortunately, the fire of passion can melt any ice. All that is necessary is for you to permit this to happen."

She felt her heart thumping. Was he talking like this because he really cared what happened to her, or was this more of his good advice for foolish youth?

Before she had time to decide, the lift arrived, and out of it stepped a slender girl in a very sophisticated green linen dress, her beautiful face expertly made up, her flame-like hair curling around her temples.

Claire stood like a statue, staring, then fell into her arms, laughing.

"Annette! Annette!"

They kissed each other, then Annette drew away and Claire felt a sudden pang of fear.

"But what are you doing here? Who's looking after Father? Annette," her voice rising in panic, "has something happened to him?"

CHAPTER EIGHT

"DON'T get worked up, Claire," Annette told her lightly, flicking a slender finger at her. "Dad's fine!"

"Then why are you here? Has he sent you to bring me home?"

Annette looked past her at the silent figure in the well-cut lounge suit whose grey eyes had been thoughtfully appraising them both during the last few minutes.

"You're not a child, Claire. You can go home whenever you're ready. Look, we'll talk later. Aren't you going to introduce your companion?" And the green eyes smiled at Louis with inviting admiration.

Claire looked round at him, having forgotten that he was even present. "Oh! Oh, yes, of course."

She performed the introduction stiffly, and Louis bent over Annette's extended hand with charming gallantry, his mouth just brushing the smooth skin.

Annette appeared to be delighted, and laughed softly. "I'm not used to having my hand kissed. It's certainly a charming custom. I wish our Englishmen would adopt it, *monsieur*."

"Please," he begged, "call me Louis. We are almost related, and it seems strange to be so formal. Even Claire has become accustomed to using my first name by now."

Annette glanced at Claire, her green eyes curious.

"I should love to use your first name, Louis, if you will use mine! But how are we related? I didn't know Madeleine had a brother. Or are you a cousin?"

"Neither," he admitted. "I am Jean-Paul's god-father."

"Jean-Paul?" She looked puzzled, then her face cleared. "Oh, that's Paul's little boy, isn't it? I'd forgotten his name."

Claire was restless and uneasy. "Louis, will you excuse us now? I must talk to Annette in private."

He bowed, regarding her with concerned grey eyes. "Of course! And if there is anything I can do, Claire, please do not hesitate to get in touch with me."

She smiled, a little distractedly, walked towards her suite. Annette reluctantly moved after her, but turned to smile back at Louis.

"I hope we'll meet again later. I'm very impressed with your hotel. It's very exciting."

He bowed politely and disappeared into the lift. Claire opened the door of her suite and went in first. Annette came in, halted, stared and gave an exclamation of amazed pleasure.

"What a fantastic place! And you're staying here free! Why did I let you come to France? I should have come myself! No wonder you aren't in a hurry to come home. Who would be with a place like this to enjoy?"

"I would have come home at once if I could have persuaded Madame Treboul to let the children come with me," Claire retorted, stung by what she saw as an accusation.

Annette laughed. "There's no need to feel guilty!

I don't blame you. After Trevillion, this must seem like heaven to you."

Claire drew a sharp breath to deny it, then shrugged. What was the point?

"Never mind all that," she said. "Tell me, why have you left Dad? Who's looking after him?"

Annette sank into one of the luxurious chairs, stretching her arms over her head so that the green linen gently outlined the grace of her figure.

"Mrs. Dillon is looking after him," she said lightly. "He's out of bed now, and taking a little exercise every day. The doctor agrees that he can slowly return to normal." She smiled at Claire. "In fact, he says there's no reason why Dad shouldn't last for another half century, so long as he doesn't do anything silly. He can work for an hour or two in a few weeks, and gradually increase the time until he's back to normal."

"That's a relief," Claire sighed. "But I still don't see why you're here."

"I had a row with Mrs. Dillon," Annette said cheerfully. "And Dad took her side, so I packed my bags and left. To tell you the truth, Claire, I have an uneasy feeling that if you don't go home soon, you'll find Mrs. Dillon a permanent fixture!"

Claire blinked. "How do you mean?"

"Use your intelligence," Annette advised. "She's Dad's age, and they get on like a house on fire. While she's been nursing him she's been persuading him that he needs a working partner—her son, in other words— and Dad told me himself that he's thinking of joining the two farms into one. Mrs. Dillon even hinted that she might marry Dad. Of course, Dad doesn't see how her mind works. Men never understand women. But the danger is there, all right."

Claire laughed. She just could not believe it. "You must be imagining things! Mrs. Dillon and Dad! Why, they've known each other for years, and I've never seen anything like that between them."

Annette eyed her pityingly. "She's right in the house now. It's been murder this week. She was running the whole place. I wasn't allowed to do a thing. If I tried to help she kindly told me to go and amuse myself. I wasn't good enough to do anything more than lay the table. My cooking was ghastly. She said I made beds as though I wanted to torture their occupants. I didn't polish the furniture hard enough, and I broke things when I washed up."

Claire laughed. Annette had never been very keen on housework and Claire could well believe that Mrs. Dillon might feel she was not much use in the home.

"All the same," she said aloud, "I still can't believe that Dad would marry Mrs. Dillon."

"Maybe not," Annette said cynically, "but I'm pretty sure she means to marry him, and that's all that's necessary. Dad couldn't escape her if he wanted to. You know how grim he's been since Paul married! Well, Mrs. Dillon and he play cards for hours, and I used to hear Dad laughing quite cheerfully."

Claire was stricken dumb by this news. Her father playing cards and laughing! He had not relaxed like that for years. She stared at her sister in disbelief.

Annette met her gaze. "Fantastic, isn't it? I told myself I was dreaming at first, but I soon saw I was right, Mrs. Dillon couldn't pull the wool over my eyes!"

"It might be just the thing for him," Claire said slowly, her mind revolving around the idea, adjusting to it. "It would be a new interest. He's always got on with Peter. I often used to think it was a pity Peter wasn't his son, since Peter saw life so much as Dad did."

Annette looked scornful. "Peter Dillon is as dull as ditchwater. He's quite content to go on working twelve hours a day on his farm for the rest of his life. He bored me to tears."

Claire looked at her, wondering if Annette had really been interested in Peter. She had fancied so, but perhaps she had been wrong. Mrs. Dillon would have seen to it that Peter kept clear of Annette. Mrs. Dillon was a woman who hung on to people and things. That was a bad thing in a mother, but in a wife? Claire could not quite visualise her father married to Mrs. Dillon, but if he did marry her, Mrs. Dillon would make him a wonderful wife.

She was so very capable and hard-working. Trevillion would get a new lease of life. Claire had done the best she could, she had worked hard, but she knew that she was not in Mrs. Dillon's class as a home-maker.

"You'll go home now, won't you?" Annette's voice made her jump. She looked at her, dark blue eyes wide and questioning.

"I'm not sure." Her sudden return home might do damage to a delicate situation. If it was really possible that her father might marry Mrs. Dillon, it might be wisest to stay away, and give them time to settle matters between them.

Annette laughed angrily. "You must, Claire! Don't you see? That woman will persuade Dad to hand Trevillion over to her son. You'll be left out in the cold. You've worked hard for Trevillion for years. What will you do if they marry? You'll lose your home. Because I know that woman—she won't want you around. She's the excluding sort."

Claire nodded. "Possessive. Yes, I know. But is it right for Dad? That's all that matters." She felt a passing pang at the thought of being excluded from Trevillion, but at the same time there was a small, faint hope. She had spent the years of her girlhood doing her duty, lovingly and willingly, but surely it was not selfish to be glad at the thought that soon she might be released from her task? She would not have walked out on her father under any other circumstances, but a new wife, a new son, a new hope for Trevillion—weren't they reason enough to be glad for herself and her father?

"Don't you care?" Annette was apparently incredulous. "You're prepared to let that woman take over our home? Claire, you can't let this happen. I couldn't do anything, but if you go home, Dad will listen to you. He loves you, he knows he owes you a lot. He wouldn't bring another woman into your home if you asked him not to."

Claire felt her cheeks sting bright red. She looked at her sister with angry, disbelieving eyes. "I would never do that! Dad doesn't owe me a thing. I stayed at Trevillion voluntarily. But it would be as wrong for me to try to hang on to Dad as it is for Mrs. Dillon to hang on to Peter."

Annette's eyes narrowed, their slanting green shining at her. "I get it! You and Peter can get married if Mrs. Dillon has other interests, and so it doesn't matter about Trevillion. It will come to the two of you, anyway. I always thought you were rather soft in the head, Claire, but I see I had you wrong. You're quite smart, in your own way!"

Claire flinched, and looked her angry disgust. "I have no intention of marrying Peter Dillon, and as for the rest of your nasty remarks, I shall ignore them!"

Annette laughed unpleasantly. "Have you got other irons in the fire, then, Claire? Like the handsome Louis? I read your letters to Dad. You got quite lyrical about Louis de Carceron at times, even though you pretended to dislike him! Mrs. Dillon thought so, too. She said as much to Dad." Annette stood up, smoothing down her dress, her eyes sharp. "In fact, I think that that was when Dad started to get friendly with Mrs. Dillon. Maybe they both decided that if you were falling in love and might get married, it would be plain sailing for them."

Claire was trembling, her hands curled at her sides, the nails digging into her palms in an effort to keep back tears of rage and humiliation. "Why do you always make things sound so horrid, Annette? You have a nasty way of putting things!"

"I just see a lot straighter than other people," Annette shrugged. "Business life teaches you to keep your eyes open and assess people's motives accurately."

"No," Claire shook her head. "You see things

through dark glasses. There are always maggots in the reddest apple for you, Annette."

"Better than walking about with your eyes shut," Annette said easily. "I never fall into pits, anyway."

"You never climb mountains, either," Claire said a little sadly. "Because for you the mountains don't exist. Your eyes are always on the ground, looking for pits. If you lifted them just once, Annette, you would have a revelation."

Annette gave her an uneasy, resentful glance. "Simple little soul, aren't you, Claire? Or so you'd have us believe. Well, let matters drift, then, let Dad marry Mrs. Dillon. But don't blame me if you regret it later."

"It won't matter if I do," Claire said. "It's not my business to interfere. Dad is an adult—let him choose. I shall be happy for him. He hasn't been very happy since Mum died. Maybe this is what he needs, a wife in his home again—a family feeling."

"Mrs. Dillon in Mum's place?" Annette's voice was shrill. "You could bear that?"

Claire looked surprised. "She wouldn't take Mum's place. No one could do that. Mrs. Dillon would make her own place."

Annette groaned. "For God's sake! Let's drop it. Where can I sleep? I presume there's room in this palatial suite?"

Claire nodded. "I have a double bed. We can share that."

"A double bed? Couldn't we have it changed to twin beds? They must be prepared for such changes, in a place like this. I'll ask Louis."

Claire did not answer, and Annette smiled sardonically at her. "I must say, I admire your taste, Claire. And all's fair in love and war, you know! He must be very rich to own a hotel like this. And didn't you mention a chateau in the Loire Valley?"

"When does your boss get back from America?" Claire asked her.

Annette shrugged. "I have ten days before he flies back. I shall stay here until then." She put a hand to her curling red hair. "And I shan't waste my time, I assure you!"

Claire felt a sinking in her stomach. She watched as Annette strolled around the suite, investigating everything with bright, pleased eyes.

"I suppose there's no competition?" Annette called from the bedroom.

"Competition?" Claire was bewildered.

"For Louis! I mean, are you my only rival? There are no other possible contenders in the area?"

Claire shivered. "I believe he's unofficially engaged," she said flatly.

Annette appeared in the bedroom door, her slender figure taut, green eyes flashing across the room at her sister. "Did you say engaged?"

Claire nodded. "To a local woman, Marise Brisseut. It's one of those arranged matches, a sort of business merger. Her family are wealthy."

"What's she like?"

"Sophisticated. Beautiful, in an austere sort of fashion." Claire heard her own voice fall dully on each word.

"How old?" Annette's voice was crisp and determined.

Claire shrugged. "Late twenties, I would say."

The red mouth tightened. "Well, let battle commence! It will be amusing, anyway. I was sick to death of Trevillion. I don't know how you put up with it. The whole house smells of damp and there's nothing to do but work." She wandered back into the bedroom. "Bring my case through, there's a dear. I'm going to take a shower and change for dinner."

Claire carried Annette's large leather case into the bedroom and heard her humming in the bathroom.

"Unpack for me, will you?" Annette called. "Lay out the white dress and the maxi slip. And make sure the other dresses are hung up properly. Can I have them pressed in the hotel? I hate creased clothes."

Claire began to unpack, sighing as she laid out a full-length white chiffon dress, cut on classical lines, with a halter neckline and straight, soft folds. Annette had come prepared, unlike herself. Her wardrobe was extensive and expensive. She would fit beautifully into the scene here at the Hotel St. Hilaire.

The telephone rang. She answered it and felt an electric jolt as she realised that it was Louis.

"Now you know why I said you would not leave," he told her.

"You knew Annette was arriving?"

"She had sent you a telegram. I opened it because I thought it might contain bad news."

"Why didn't you tell me?"

He did not answer for a moment. Then, "You were in a very aggressive mood. I wanted you to surrender

148

on my terms for once." Another pause, and then he added coolly, "Which you did! I would have told you later. I did not expect her to arrive so soon."

Claire said unevenly, "Yes, she was a surprise."

He asked quickly, "She brought you bad news?"

"No," she said, considering the answer. "No, I don't think so."

"You do not sound sure! Is she staying?"

"Yes, apparently she is. She wanted to ask if you could change the bed for two twin beds."

"Of course, at once. I will put it in hand. Will you both dine with me?"

Claire sighed. "Thank you."

"You might try to sound less resigned," he snapped. "Is it such a bore to dine with me, Claire?"

"I'm sorry. It wasn't that."

"Something is causing you anxiety?" Now his voice was concerned and gentle. "Tell me about it."

"No," she said flatly. "We will see you at eight, then." And hung up.

She turned and saw Annette, enveloped in a huge lemon towel, her flame-coloured hair rolled back under a cap, watching her from the bathroom door.

"That was him, wasn't it? You give yourself away with every word, do you know that? It must be embarrassing for him."

"He wants us to have dinner with him at eight," Claire said, ignoring her last remarks.

Annette nodded. "I gathered that much. What else did he have to say?"

Claire walked towards the door of the suite. "Nothing important. I'll see you later."

"Where are you going?"

"Out for a walk," said Claire, closing the door behind her.

She found herself on the beach, walking slowly through the last few sunbathers, her thoughts engrossing her total attention. It was bitter to think that her love for Louis was so obvious that Annette had seen it at once. Had Louis also noticed it? She shivered, a coldness running over her skin.

Even if Louis had no idea, she thought, Annette's arrival changed things. She could not compete with her sister for Louis's attention. It was a degrading situation. Why had Annette come here? Had her revealing letters made her sister curious? Had she come deliberately to see Louis?

The sun was sinking, the beach was rapidly becoming deserted as one by one the bathers gathered up their belongings and made their way home. Claire still walked, her eyes on the darkening sky, thinking about her father, Trevillion, the two children, the unknown future. What would she do now? Suppose her father did marry Mrs. Dillon? She would get a job somewhere. London? But she had had no training. What could she do?

She made her way back to the hotel. The suite was empty. Annette's belongings were strewn everywhere, in disorder, traces of talc scattered on the pink carpet, a heavy scent of perfume hanging in the room. Claire sighed and began to tidy up. She could not leave the room like this for the maid to find. When she had restored it to some sort of order, she hurriedly changed into her black dress and went back to reception.

She bumped into Pierre, who smiled and told her that Annette was with Louis in the bar.

"She is *ravissante*, your sister! *Très belle et très chic*!" He spread his shoulders in one of those meaningful shrugs. "But hard, no? I would not want Léon to marry such as that one!"

She laughed at his English, and walked through into the bar, where she paused, watching the three people in the corner with apprehension.

Louis was lighting a cigarette for Annette, his grey glance admiringly fixed on those red lips. Annette leaned towards him, revealing white shoulders and the eloquent line of throat and breast, her slanting green eyes sparkling into his, her hand lightly touching his as he held his cigarette lighter for her.

Beside them, sleek and self-possessed, sat Marise Brisseut, in an exquisitely simple grey dress which emphasised the glowing olive skin, black hair and dark eyes.

As Louis leaned back, smiling, Annette's slanting eyes slid sideways and challenged Marise, a triumphant, feline smile on her mouth.

A splinter of ice penetrated the dullness around Claire's heart. How could they behave like this? Louis sat, lightly swinging one polished shoe, speaking somewhere between them, apparently unconscious of the atmosphere. Did he accept their jealous competition as his due? Or was he really unaware of the narrowed eyes, secret looks and eager display?

He turned at that moment, saw her and for a second their eyes met. His were cold, steely. The thin nostrils quivered with rage. Why? she wondered without real curiosity. What had she done to annoy him now?

He crossed the space between them, took her elbow to tightly that a sting of pain made her jerk away, and looked down into her face, his shoulder turned so that the other two could not see his expression.

"So, you arrive at last! That is very gracious of you! You do not intend, I suppose, to apologise for being unpunctual?"

"I'm sorry," she said flatly. "I forgot the time."

He raised one thin brow. "What were you doing? Annette said you vanished while she was bathing."

"I went for a walk." Claire stared at the carpet, tracing the coiled pattern of dark gold and black without interest.

"You were disturbed by her news?" he asked quickly. "You are concerned about this Peter Dillon? Annette has told me that you and he are very close."

A wry smile twisted Claire's lips. Annette was wasting no time!

When she did not reply, Louis's hand tightened on her arm. "You do not deny it? This was a boy and girl affair, no?" His accent had thickened and become much more French. "Such a relationship is often merely habit. It is wise to consider whether we are accepting second best when we take the easiest course. If you had really loved this young man you would have married him long ago."

She sighed. She wished he would keep his no doubt well-meant advice to himself. He was the last man in the world to whom she could listen on such a subject.

He waited a moment, then said tightly, "And you

will never hang up on me again! I will not tolerate such deliberate ill manners!"

Claire raised her head, dazed and uncomprehending. The wide dark blue eyes looked into his with a childlike bewilderment. "Hang up?"

"When I spoke to you earlier on the telephone, you hung up without a word. Do not pretend you did not do so deliberately. You did not wish to discuss Annette's news with me."

A sudden suspicion darted into her mind. "What has Annette told you?"

He stared at her. "Why, that this Peter Dillon may soon marry someone else, and that you are eager to return home to make sure he does not do so. Is this not so?"

She looked past him at Annette. Her sister was watching them, green eyes alert and narrowed. How could Annette do this?

"I'll go home when I'm ready to do so," she said, evading the issue.

"What are you two talking about?" Annette joined them, giving Claire a hard, probing glance. She slipped her hand through Louis's arm, smiling up at him. "You mustn't neglect your other guests, Louis! Are we going in to dinner now that Claire has got over the shock about Peter?" She slid a sidelong look at Claire, as if to check that her sister had not denied the truth of her fairy tale.

Claire met her eyes scornfully. Annette hurriedly looked away.

"Yes," Louis was saying, "we will go in to dinner

now." He took Marise on his other arm and turned towards the door.

Claire followed, feeling forlorn. The fact that Louis could be deliberately discourteous towards her was sufficient proof that their unstable relationship had slumped to a new low. Only some really serious reaction could have made him ignore her like this.

Over dinner, she watched the two other women blatantly jockeying for position. Little, feline remarks; sharp looks, discreetly veiled triumph whenever Louis seemed to favour one or the other. It was a sickening exhibition, Claire thought.

It was while they were drinking their coffee that Louis mentioned Le Petit Trésor. Giving Claire a brief, unrevealing look, he told Annette that he hoped she would join the guests at his home.

"We leave in two days' time," he added.

Annette looked delighted. "Why, I would adore it! How very kind of you, Louis!"

Marise leaned towards him. "Are you sure it is wise to take such a large party, Louis? How will Agathe cope with such an influx?"

Annette laughed sweetly. "Claire will be delighted to help your servants, Louis! Won't you, Claire? She's so domesticated!"

Louis's jaw was angular, his steely gaze fixed on his cup. "Claire will not do domestic work at Le Petit Trésor!" There was a little silence, then he added lightly, "We are all on holiday. Agathe will manage. She can get help from the village."

CHAPTER NINE

THEY travelled in two cars. Louis took Marise and Annette with him, while Claire sat with the two children in the back of Monsieur Treboul's black saloon. Madame had prepared a vast hamper of food and drink, which she distributed during the journey, watching with fond indulgence as Marie-Claire carelessly nibbled a piece of chicken and crunched on crisps.

Claire played a game with them to keep them happy. They each looked out of the window on their side of the car and called out excitedly whenever they saw a red car. There was a small prize for the one who got the highest number of red cars, and Claire was the referee.

Jean-Paul won by default, in the end, since his little sister slowly fell asleep long before the end of the game. Biting reflectively into his prize, a chocolate bar, Jean-Paul told Claire that his sister was a baby.

"I am a big boy," he insisted proudly.

The two parties were to meet again half way, at the roadside *auberge* which Louis had decided would be a good place to take a meal. Claire stayed in the car with the two children. The hamper Madame Treboul had provided had been more than sufficient for them, and she too was not hungry. Marie-Claire was fast asleep, her head on Claire's shoulder. Jean-

Paul was drowsy but obstinately determined to stay awake at all costs. Madame and Monsieur Treboul joined the others and disappeared into the *auberge*.

Louis came out a few moments later with a glass of red wine for Claire.

"You will drink this," he stated sternly.

She accepted it reluctantly, expecting him to go, but he stood, watching her while she sipped, his dark face inscrutable.

"Jean-Paul," he said, "you should stretch your legs while you can. Go for a stroll around the garden."

Jean-Paul was ready to do so, and Claire watched him skipping between neat flower beds alongside the grey walls of the auberge.

"You look tired," Louis told her suddenly. "It has been a strain, this journey? The children are tiring. Madame has told me that you have much patience with them, but she feels you need a break. You will come in my car for the next part of our journey and Annette shall get to know the children."

Claire wondered what Annette would say to that. She could imagine how her sister would greet the news.

Aloud, she said, "Thank you, but I don't find the children tiring. They're used to me. I'll stay with them."

He stood upright, his mouth a thin line. "You refuse?"

"It was very kind of you, but . . ."

"But you refuse!" He turned and walked away without another word.

Now he was angry again, Claire thought, with

desolation. Why was he so difficult? It seemed almost as if they were fated to be at loggerheads for ever.

Marie-Claire woke up, yawning, and Claire took her for a stroll in the garden. They played hide and seek with Jean-Paul for ten minutes, and then found the cloakroom and had their sticky little faces washed, their hair combed and their clothes brushed down to dislodge the crumbs from their picnic.

It was late in the afternoon when they arrived at Le Petit Trésor. They drove down one of the straight poplar-lined roads, turned off into a narrow track and found themselves at a pair of wrought iron gates. These led into a broad drive, shaded by lime trees, which curved round in front of an exquisite little house, built in the classical eighteenth-century style, with white portico and flat, perfectly proportioned windows.

Louis, Marise and Annette stood on the path, looking up at the house. Madame, Monsieur, Claire and the children joined them.

"But I thought it was a chateau," Annette said in disappointed tones.

Claire was silent, her eyes delightedly searching the pure, delicate lines of window and roof, the elegant scrollwork above the windows, the glossy white door, with its gold, lion-headed knocker.

The door opened and an old woman came bustling out, clad in the usual black, with a white apron and collar, her grey hair worn rigidly on the back of her small head, nailed there, it seemed, by huge pins.

"Agathe!" Louis embraced her fondly, kissing either cheek. A tall, smiling, clumsy young man in

157

rough jersey and brown corduroy trousers followed her and began to take in the luggage.

Agathe looked at the guests, greeted Madame Treboul with a sharp smile and a nod, gave the two children a softened glance, let her black eyes rest on Claire for a second, taking in the way the two children leaned sleepily against her. Then she looked at the other two women, sniffed loudly and hobbled back into the house.

Louis led his guests up the steps into the elegant little hall. Agathe was waiting, hands folded over her apron.

"Agathe will show you to your rooms," Louis said politely.

They all trooped up the wide, curving staircase. Claire carried Marie-Claire, held Jean-Paul's hot little hand tightly.

Agathe paused on the landing and looked at her. "The nursery is up there," she said, pointing to a further flight.

Claire nodded and followed the stairs wearily. At the top she found a door, fumbled, pushed it open and then stopped in surprised delight at what she saw.

The room was octagonal, the walls more than half window, with thick green curtains drawn over them. Felt animals were sewn on the curtains. Pink pigs, white ducks, yellow chicks, marched across in uneven lines. Two little beds were pushed close together, their covers matching the curtains. Beside a roaring fire stood an armchair and a shaded lamp.

Claire sat Marie-Claire on one of the beds and explored into a further room, which turned out to be a bathroom. She came back and led the two children into it. Their case stood beside the beds. She unpacked their pyjamas, washed them and dressed them. They were curled up in bed, fast asleep, ten minutes later.

Claire turned out the central light, sat down in the armchair and stared into the fire. The room was warm and cosy, the sound of the children's breath the only sound to break the silence, except for the gentle ticking of the clock and the occasional sound of ash dropping down from the fire.

She hardly noticed the passage of time. Content and relaxed, she nodded against the back of the chair, smiling whenever her eyes fell upon those two tiny bodies beneath their warm covers.

The fire slowly died, but the room remained warm. It was summer, but presumably Agathe had been worried about the possibility of damp in the unused nursery. Had this been Louis's nursery? Had he slept in one of these little beds, following the procession of felt animals across the curtains? She could not imagine it. What sort of child had he been? Domineering, confident, clever? Had he ever been lonely or sad? She knew so little of him.

Louis was an unreadable mystery to her. That dark face, the glittering grey eyes, revealed nothing of what he thought, except when anger dominated him, and even then she rarely understood what had made him angry.

She hardly noticed her consciousness slipping away. Her eyes drooped for the last time, her head slumped against the chair.

Suddenly a hand touched her, and she jerked

awake, hardly aware of her surroundings, eyes blinking, dazzled by the soft light. She looked up into Louis's face and consciousness hit her. She felt herself gathering up her last fragments of self-control, a shutter slipped down between them, hiding from him whatever she might have revealed by one unaware glance.

"It is late, Claire," he said unevenly. "You must go to your own room. Agathe will be sleeping next door, if the children awake. I will make sure that the fire is out before I leave them."

She stood up, her legs unsteady. He caught her waist and held her. Something rose in her throat, suffocating, demanding, terrifying.

She moved away hurriedly, pushing at her hair. "I . . . I don't know where I'm sleeping," she said nervously.

"I will show you," he said.

He led her down the stairs, pointed out a door and turned to leave her. Claire paused, suddenly torn by a longing so intense that she could hardly bear it. She was still half dazed with sleep, her resistance low.

Louis glanced back, saw indecision shifting over her features, and said quickly, "Something is wrong, Claire?"

The sound of his voice snapped her back into reality. "No," she said swiftly, and went into her room.

She put on the light, closed the door and leaned against it, then stared in amazement. Marise Brisseut was sitting on her bed, smoking a cigarette, her dark red velvet dressing-gown open to reveal a shimmering white nightgown.

She regarded Claire, one brow raised. "You have finished your duties for tonight? Good! I want a word with you, Mademoiselle Stratton."

The husky voice was a little contemptuous, Claire noted. She came forward and contemplated Marise wearily.

"I'm tired. Can't this wait until morning?"

"No! I want to make sure you understand me." Marise stubbed her cigarette out, with a violent gesture, on a small china ashtray beside her. Then she lit another at once, drew on it and let her dark eyes wander over Claire's dishevelled hair and dress.

"This sister of yours—she must return to England!"

Claire was stunned into laughter. Marise glared at her, the red mouth showing small white teeth.

"It is not amusing! She is a nuisance! Her open and shameless pursuit of Louis embarrasses him, yet he feels that he must be polite to her, since she is related to the Trebouls. It is for you to persuade her to leave."

"I can't do that," Claire said.

"You will do it," Marise stated confidently. "Or I shall go to Madame Treboul and get her to do it. Madame knows how much I need to marry Louis. She is as eager as the rest of my family. You know, perhaps, that my sister is Marie-Claire's godmother. Family loyalty will ensure that Madame intervenes on my behalf."

Claire's mind was not working very well at the moment. She was too tired.

"What makes you think that Annette will listen to

Madame any more than to me? Annette is a free agent. She listens to nobody but herself."

Marise smiled glitteringly. "Madame will not speak to Annette. She will speak to you, and forbid you to see the children again. She will refuse to let them visit your father, or to allow him to visit them."

Claire paled and trembled. She could not believe her ears. "Madame would never consent to such a cruel piece of blackmail," she said.

Marise shrugged. "You do not know her very well. To have Louis de Carceron as a part of our family she would do anything! All the family agree to this. It is an ambition realised. Of course, Madame would be sad to do it, but . . ." she gestured, "one must be prepared to be ruthless in the pursuit of one's ambition."

Claire was wide awake now. White-faced and angry, she asked in a low tone, "And what about Tony Kirk? Was he a sacrifice to your ruthless ambition?"

Marise sat up, her cigarette in her hand, her eyes narrowed. "So! You know about that!"

Claire stared at her scornfully. "Tony told me about it. You let him think you wanted to marry him, then ditched him for Louis. Why did you change your mind about marrying Louis? Or were you just lying to Tony from the beginning?"

Marise smoked in silence for a moment, then walked restlessly around the room. "I did not lie to Tony! Circumstances changed."

"What circumstances?"

Marise glanced at her dubiously. "My father lost a great deal of money," she said at last. "Once it was just a pretty idea, for me to marry Louis. Now it is essential, not just for myself, but for my father."

"Then you did care for Tony?" Claire probed, watching her.

Marise shrugged. "That is my business. It is out of the question now, however, and so, irrelevant." She swung round on Claire, her black eyes shining like a tiger's. "And you! You were interested in Tony, were you not? Louis confided to me that it worried him to see an innocent young girl striking up a friendship with someone so experienced as Tony!" She smiled fiercely, the red lips curling. "You found Tony's experience charming, no doubt? Little innocents often find such a man irresistible. It is his lightness of manner that attracts you? His freedom?" Her eyes grew abstracted, and she spoke almost to herself. "He is not a man easy to cage. He lacks ambition and is too cynical. That is the challenge! To make such a man care . . . care violently. . . ." She sighed thickly, her eyes sensuous and hungry. "But it is useless when one has other needs."

Claire had made a discovery. She watched Marise carefully. Yes, the woman was in love—and with Tony! It had been unmistakable when Marise spoke about making him care violently. Hunger had stared out of her black eyes.

Marise turned back to her, pushing aside the subject of Tony. "But you will speak to your sister? If you do not persuade her to go back to England, I shall have to approach Madame Treboul. I do not want to do this, but I will do what I must."

"Nothing I can say will sway my sister," Claire said.

Marise looked angry. "You will think of something!"

"And suppose I tell Louis what I know about you and Tony?" Claire asked quietly.

Marise stared hard at her. "You will not! Louis believes that it was you who was in love with Tony. He will not believe a wild story about me." She walked to the door. "Think about what I have said. I want to be rid of your troublesome sister as soon as possible."

Surprisingly, Claire slept deeply that night. She had grown too close to Madame to believe that she would carry out Marise's cruel threat.

Agathe had a girl from the village to help her with the harder duties of running the house. Claire found the girl busy cleaning the pans in the kitchen when she went down to fetch the two children's breakfast next morning. Agathe came in as Claire was carrying up a tray neatly laid with boiled eggs, fruit juice and warm milk.

The thin, wrinkled old face broke into a smile. "*Bonjour, ma petite!*"

Claire replied eagerly. Agathe had been Louis's nurse when he was little. She must know him better than anyone else. Claire wondered how Agathe regarded Marise.

The old woman inspected the tray and nodded approval. "I shall come up to help you with the little ones later," she said, as Claire went out.

Jean-Paul was lively this morning, his face cheeky and eager to be exploring this new place. When they had eaten their breakfasts and washed, Claire got them ready to go out. She had eaten her coffee and fruit with them and had promised to take them for a walk.

Madame and Monsieur came in, bade them a loving good morning, and listened indulgently to Jean-Paul's plans for the day.

"Claire will take us to see the fountains, first, then we go to see the vines." His face clouded. "How Miel would have loved to run about in the garden! Why did we not bring him?"

"I have told you, *mon petit*," said Madame, "little dogs do not go on holiday. Miel will be waiting when we get back."

Jean-Paul sighed, but even the absence of his beloved puppy could not spoil the radiance of the day. He seized Claire's hand. "Come, *ma tante*, we explore, no?"

Madame looked sharply into Claire's rather pale face. "You are well, *ma petite*?"

Claire smiled, warmed by the use of the personal "*tu*", which is only used inside the family in France.

"Perfectly well, thank you. A little tired, perhaps, after our journey yesterday."

Monsieur studied her seriously. "I do not like to see dark shadows under young eyes," he said gently. "Something worries you, my dear Claire?"

She shook her head and forced another smile, then followed Jean-Paul out of the room.

The gardens lay around the chateau in smooth, rolling green curves. A formal French garden, laid out with ornate stone walls and fountains, faced the front of the house. Jean-Paul roamed around excitedly while Marie-Claire clung to her aunt's hand, half frightened by the white spears of water which were flung up at her from time to time from the cupped hands of a nymph posed to dive into the round pond. Jean-Paul wandered through into the gentle landscape of an English garden, laid out with oaks and shady elms, the centre fragrant with lavender, roses and carnations growing in an enclosed sunken circle. The warm red walls seemed to throw back the scent of the flowers, holding the sun's heat.

Claire looked back at the elegant façade of the house. It must have been wonderful to live here in the early days, when the rooms were full of ladies in silken gowns and gentlemen in lace cravats.

Jean-Paul was now eager to visit the vineyard, but Claire decided that Marie-Claire had had enough for one morning, so she promised to take the little boy there after lunch, and slowly led them back to the house.

They met Louis as they went back. He bowed gallantly to Marie-Claire and picked her up, holding her easily on one shoulder, where she giggled and clutched at his sleek black hair, throwing it into wild disarray.

The grey eyes looked down at Claire, studying her face. "You have enjoyed your walk around my gardens?"

"We saw fountains," Jean-Paul announced excitedly. "And after lunch we go to the vineyard!"

Louis raised a dark brow. "So? I think I will accompany you, *mon petit*. I do not want to have my best wine sampled by a connoisseur like yourself!"

Jean-Paul giggled and pinched his hand. "You make

fun of me, *mon parrain*! Will you show us your wine cellars?"

Louis pretended to consider the question. "Hmm . . . will it be safe, I ask myself? Or will you steal my best vintages? But I will take this small risk."

Claire took the two children up to the nursery, where Agathe had already begun to lay out their lunch, on a small folding table. Dark green tablecloth, white earthenware plates and mugs, a small vase of white flowers in the centre.

"Salad? I do not like salad!" Marie-Claire was fretful, her face flushed and her eyes heavy.

"The little one is tired," Agathe pronounced with a shrewd glance. She seated Marie-Claire, served her *potage*, thick with vegetables, and spread a slice of bread with butter. Gently she fed the little girl, while Claire attended to Jean-Paul. His healthy appetite made short work of the *potage*, the salad and boiled eggs with cheese and diced ham, the *crème caramel*. He drank his milk thirstily, wiped his mouth with his napkin and asked to get down.

Agathe firmly put both children to bed and whispered to Claire to leave them with her while she joined the rest of the guests for lunch.

Claire hesitated. If Agathe was up here, who would be doing the work downstairs?

Agathe smiled, her dark eyes disappearing among her wrinkles. "I have the silly Léonie to serve at table! It is only salad, also. Go, *ma petite* . . . eat your lunch with a clear conscience!"

Claire went to her own room, washed and brushed her hair, then went down into the dining-room, where she found the others waiting for her. She slipped into the empty chair, flushing. "I'm sorry!"

Madame said gently, "We knew that you were attending to *les enfants, ma petite*. Do not concern yourself. We are happy to wait for you."

"We are grateful that you look after them," Monsieur added, beaming at her.

Marise broke a croissant with an angry snap. "It was, my dear Louis, a little mistaken, perhaps, to bring the children. They are a little too young, I think, for such a long journey."

Madame looked at her, brows drawing together in a heavy frown. "But, my dear Marise, the whole idea of this trip was for Claire to see the chateau while she was in France, and obviously she did not want to leave the children behind. She has said that she wishes to see as much of them as she can!" She glanced at Claire. "Is it not so, *ma petite*?"

Claire nodded nervously, aware that Marise was eyeing her with a menacing irritation. "Yes, I wouldn't have come without the children."

Louis broke in harshly, "Come, we are letting this excellent *potage* grow cold!" He lifted a small bell and rang it, and the maid came forward to serve the *potage*. She went carefully from one to the other, ladling out the thick liquid. Marise leaned back as the girl reached her, jogging the maid's arm, and *potage* spilled on to her skirt.

White and furious, she made a brief exclamation. "Clumsy fool!" The vicious tone made the girl whiten and stumble back.

Louis was on his feet at once, smoothing Marise

down, rubbing gently at the damp stain with a handkerchief.

"Go on serving, Léonie," he ordered the maid, not unkindly. "But be careful!"

She finished serving and gratefully withdrew. Marise ate her meal in a sullen silence. They had the same meal as the children, if more plentiful, and withdrew to the small salon to drink their coffee.

The salon was an elegant little room, a cool mixture of white and green, with gilding on the door panels and some of the eighteenth-century furniture. A brocade-covered chaise-longue, two armchairs and a matching sofa were arranged for conversation around the room.

Claire watched with embarrassment as both Annette and Marise hastened to take up a position on the chaise-longue.

Louis was too swift for them, however. Calmly, politely, he smiled and told them that Madame should have the chaise-longue, since she always slept after lunch, and could sleep on undisturbed when they had gone elsewhere.

Monsieur drank his coffee and made his exit, regretfully explaining that he must take his little nap or he would not last out the day. Annette sat at one end of the sofa, Marise at the other, holding their coffee cups and smiling invitingly at Louis, who had stationed himself impartially upon the hearth.

Claire endured the difficult conversation for ten minutes, then rose, excusing herself to join the children. Let Annette and Marise fight it out between them, she decided, slipping upstairs to the nursery.

Agathe was seated in the armchair, quietly sewing at a dainty white object, while the children slept deeply, with rosy pink faces and tousled hair. Claire tiptoed in, smiled at Agathe and gestured to her that she could now leave the watch to her.

Agathe rose, folded her sewing, smiled and departed on silent feet.

Claire watched the children broodingly. How sweet they looked now, even the lively Jean-Paul curled round like a little dormouse, his lids shut tightly in dreams. It was going to be very hard to leave them. She had grown very fond of them in these few days. She saw so many little signs of her brother in Jean-Paul. And Marie-Claire had such a lovely, appealing little face.

She became alert as the little girl stirred, gave a choked cry. Claire moved to her side and bent over her. Marie-Claire's thick lashes fluttered. A small tear rolled down the baby cheek. Claire felt a sharp pain around her heart. She wanted to pick the child up, cuddle her back to happiness.

Gently she touched the pink cheek. Marie-Claire lay still, lids still closed, then her little mouth formed the word, "Maman?" And Claire felt hot salt tears spring into her own eyes, a sob catch in her throat.

"*Ma petite. . . .*" she whispered, stroking the child's hair.

Marie-Claire sighed and lay still, her breathing once more becoming normal.

After a moment Claire turned away, and then stopped in her tracks, staring at Louis's dark face. He stood in the doorway, a hand pressed against the frame, his thin brows drawn together in a frown. They looked at each other, the tall, handsome man and the girl with straight shining hair and wet eyes, and then he turned on his heel and went out without a word.

CHAPTER TEN

JEAN-PAUL found the vineyards a little disappointing, but he brightened when they arrived at the shadowy cellars in which the best vintages were stored.

"It is mysterious, no?" Louis asked him, a little teasingly. "Will you be afraid in the dark, my little cabbage?"

"No, *mon parrain*," the little boy declared firmly. "I like it that it is dark."

"But we will take a torch, in case!" Louis decided calmly. He took Jean-Paul's hand and led him into the cool interior.

Claire followed them slowly. They had left Marie-Claire behind with Agathe, since she was not old enough for any strenuous activity. Agathe had warmly insisted that she was happy to look after the little girl, and would amuse her in the kitchen, making gingerbread men for their tea.

Claire had seen nothing of either Marise or Annette, and wondered if they were aware of Louis's visit to the vineyards with her. She had been silent during the brief tour, enjoying the warm sunshine and the long green vistas, exchanging polite greetings with the men who were working out there and who had stared curiously at herself and Jean-Paul, clearly wondering who they were.

Louis had been icily courteous to her, but she knew

that he was still angry about something. His strange moods came and went without her ever really understanding what caused them. He had been angered this time, she suspected, to see her weeping over Marie-Claire. Louis despised emotionalism. He had warned her before never to be emotional with them, and she did understand his reason for insisting upon this, but it was easier to decide to be calm and steady, and quite another to carry out such a decision in cold blood when a child was in need of comfort.

They walked down a flight of steep steps, Jean-Paul now carried in Louis's arms, and came to a high-vaulted dark room, filled to the roof with serried ranks of wine racks. Louis shone his torch over them, then switched it out.

"It is better if we look when our eyes become accustomed to the dark," he said "There is light coming into the cellar," and he gestured to a glass window let into the wall at the far end. "Soon we shall see well." He bent over Jean-Paul. "We shall see like cats in the dark, *mon choux*!"

"I shall see like a tiger," Jean-Paul claimed, growling and pretending to scratch with his claws.

"*Ciel!*" Louis moved back, pretending to be frightened. "What a terrifying animal!"

Claire laughed softly. It was enchanting to be here with them, to hear Louis playing with the little boy in that gay, light-hearted way. It made him seem a different person, younger, less alarming, more approachable.

She felt rather than saw him look round at her. Jean-Paul was moving away, growlingly inspecting the wine racks. "I see spiders," she heard him saying to himself. "Good! Tigers eat spiders!"

Louis was close beside her now. Her heart began to thud in that slow, heavy way to which she had become accustomed whenever he was near her. She wondered if he could hear it, and instinctively moved back a little, coming up against the brick wall of the cellar.

Louis leaned one hand against the wall so that she could not move away, and looked down at her, his eyes glittering in the shadows, his face a pale, unreadable mask.

"You are like a little frightened mouse, Claire," he said in soft, husky tones. "If it were not for that obvious fear of yours I would think that . . ." He paused, then gave a short laugh. "No, not now!" He moved away, calling Jean-Paul and began to show the boy some of the better vintages.

Claire stayed where she was, breathing fast. What had he meant? For one elating, terrifying second she had imagined he was going to kiss her, and her whole body had begun to tremble violently.

She shook herself back into some sort of calm. This was beginning to turn her brain, this deep, unbearable feeling she had for Louis! She must get away from him. She did not think she could bear much more. Her whole existence seemed to have become focused on him, excluding everything else which had ever meant anything to her.

She looked through the sea-green shadows of the cellar towards where he was standing beside Jean-Paul, holding out a dusty bottle for his inspection, and a sigh wrenched at her. It was going to be hard to leave him.

They emerged from the shadows and stood, blinking, in the brilliant sunlight. Jean-Paul pretended to be unable to see, and went spinning around wildly, laughing.

Louis smiled, but Claire ran to catch hold of the child's hand, afraid that he would hurt himself.

She heard Louis exclaim savagely, turned in surprise and stood very still, staring at the man who had just sauntered through the yard.

"Hi!" He grinned at her easily, apparently oblivious of Louis's menacing stare.

"Tony! What are you doing here?" She looked around at Louis nervously, eyes wide.

Tony shrugged casual shoulders. "I have permission to see the chateau. I intend to include it in my book."

Louis stalked up to them. "I did not expect to find you here, Kirk. I told you that you could only visit the chateau when I was not in residence."

Tony grinned at him, undismayed. "I know, *monsieur*. But I did ring your housekeeper a few days ago, and she told me you wouldn't be here until the weekend. So I came along."

Louis's nostrils were tight with rage. "And you can leave again. At once! I will not have my privacy disturbed while I am on holiday!"

Tony's smile did not falter. He looked cheerfully at Louis. "Surely, while I'm here, I can see something! I met Marise up at the house, and she said I could stay to dinner."

Louis's teeth snapped like a spring. "I cannot believe

that Marise would do so! She knows that I do not invite strangers to dine at Le Petit Trésor."

Tony shrugged, his casually rakish features still smiling. "Maybe she was sorry for me. I haven't eaten since breakfast. I wanted to get here before it was dark."

"You are not staying the night," Louis exclaimed thinly. "If Marise has invited you to dinner, you may stay, but you leave immediately afterwards. There is a comfortable inn in the village."

Tony nodded. "I know. I booked in on my way here." He grinned. "But thanks for your gracious hospitality, Monsieur de Carceron. You've really been too kind."

Louis's face grew black at the sarcasm, but he said nothing. Taking Jean-Paul by the hand he walked away, ignoring Claire.

Tony looked at her, his eyes bright. "Well, he's certainly a charming fellow! I really appreciate his welcome!"

"You shouldn't have come here," Claire said, distressed. "How could you, Tony? Feeling as you do about Marise, how can you bear to force your way into Louis's home?"

He shrugged. "I really didn't know you were all here. It was quite a shock to see Marise, I can tell you." His eyes darkened. "It shocked her, too. She went white. I think she thought I'd come to tell de Carceron the truth about her." He sighed. "I wouldn't have the guts, of course. You have to be as ruthless as my sweet Marise to do a rotten thing like that!"

Claire felt compassion stirring in her. She saw the

pain in Tony's eyes. The dullness and grief she knew so well herself.

Putting a hand on his arm, she said, "I'm sure she really cares for you, Tony. She almost admitted it to me."

He looked at her with quick, hungry hope, then sighed, shaking his head. "Why should she throw me over, then?"

She told him what Marise had told her, and he listened intently, frowning.

"So old Brisseut is short of cash? That would explain it, and I have heard rumours." He grimaced. "It makes it a little easier to bear if I tell myself Marise really feels something for me, but it doesn't alter the situation. She'll marry Louis just the same."

Claire nodded. Yes, that was true. She led the way back to the chateau and halted, seeing Marise standing in the hall, her eyes watchful.

Tony slid an arm around Claire's waist His blue eyes met those of Marise with cynical amusement.

"Well, well, if it isn't Marise!" He bowed sardonically. "I hate to admit it, *mademoiselle*, but this chateau is worth marrying the Lord High Executioner for! You'll make a lovely chatelaine, too. But Claire and I feel easier with more humble surroundings, don't we, Claire?"

Embarrassed, Claire slid away from him and moved towards the stairs. She was not going to let Tony use her to bait Marise!

She passed the sleek, black-haired woman, evading the stabbing dark eyes, and ran quickly up to the nursery, leaving the two of them confronting each other like armed enemies.

She found Annette in her room, turning in front of the mirror with her head to one side, inspecting herself with the intense absorption of the beautiful. Claire sighed. She did not feel up to another long argument on the lines of those they had had before about Louis and Marise. As she closed the door and came forward into the room, Annette looked at her in the mirror, her fingers on the curls around her temple.

"I'm leaving," she said succinctly.

Claire stared at her, not sure she had heard correctly, and her sister nodded.

"I had a telegram from my boss this afternoon. It had been following me all over the place, but it finally got to me. He's going to South America on an extended tour for six months, and he wants me to fly out there and join him in three days. I have to go back to London, make sure everything is in order there, and then catch the first available flight to New York."

Claire felt a flood of warm relief. "Have you told Louis?" she asked tentatively.

Annette's lovely face hardened. "I told him when he came back from the vineyard just now. He graciously offered to make the arrangements for me to get to London."

"Oh." Claire met the bright, angry green eyes. "Well," she pointed out reasonably, "that was kind of him. He's only known you for a few days."

"Kind?" Annette's red lips drew back in an angry smile. "He was damned rude! He practically snapped my head off when I asked him if he thought I should go. Said something about my private life being no concern of his, and in the most unpleasant voice. I've never seen him in a mood like that. I don't think I liked him so much, after all."

Claire wondered if Louis's anger had something to do with Tony's reappearance and that unfortunate invitation to dinner. Why had Marise done it? She must have known that to invite Tony to dinner would be a red rag to a bull.

Annette was considering her vivid reflection again, her slanting eyes almost fever-bright with temper. She shrugged. "Well, I've never been to South America. It will be a new experience. And the place is crawling with millionaires."

"When do you leave?" Claire asked her.

"Right away. Louis ordered a car for me. He got me a booking on a flight to London at eleven o'clock tonight." She turned and regarded Claire smoulderingly. "He couldn't wait to get rid of me!"

"Oh, I'm sure. . . ." Claire began hurriedly, but her sister cut her short.

"Forget it! I'd better say goodbye now. See you when I get back from South America. And Claire, if Mrs. Dillon does hook Dad, you can come and share my flat, you know. I'll help you get a job somewhere."

Claire felt a little catch in her throat. She hugged Annette. "Thank you. That's very kind of you."

Annette shook her head. Brusquely she said, "Kind nothing! I've always had a guilt complex about you, Claire. It was rotten to leave you to cope with Dad all those years." The green eyes looked evasively over her head. "I wouldn't blame you if you resented it."

179

"I don't," Claire said shyly. "I really had a lot of fun, you know, playing at being a housekeeper. Especially at first. And you would have hated it so much. I knew that, even then."

Annette roughly touched her shoulder. "You're a fool, Claire. When will you learn that you have to grab what you want? If you let people use you they will, you know!" She looked at her with mingled pity and irritation. "I suppose you'll let Louis marry that scheming little cat, Marise, and then you'll go away and suffer for years in silence. Grow up! If you want him, grab him. It's the only way to get what you want!"

"It . . . it still isn't my way," Claire said, half laughing, half serious. "It's not in my nature."

Annette gazed at her, shaking her head. "I suppose not! Ah, well, it takes all sorts, but I'm glad I have more initiative than you have, Claire. I've got to the top in my profession by using my brains and my will power." She smiled, flicked a finger at Claire's cheek, and was gone.

Claire went up to the nursery to see the two children bathed and put to bed. Jean-Paul was still lively, his voice cheerful as he demanded a bedtime story, but Marie-Claire was drowsy in her bed, her lashes fanned out over her soft cheek.

Claire perched on the side of the little boy's bed and told him the story of the Three Little Pigs, very softly. He laughed and bounced up and down in his bed, repeating the wolf's threat to huff and puff and blow the house down. Agathe came in and gave him a stern look.

"Now, *mon petit*, to sleep!"

"I am not sleepy! Another story, Tante Claire, another story!"

Claire smiled at Agathe, and told the child, "Tomorrow, Jean-Paul. I'll tell you the story of the Three Bears, if you're good now, and go to sleep. If not—no story tomorrow!"

He burrowed down under the bedclothes, peeping wickedly at her. "Growl . . . growl . . . I am a big bear. . . ."

She kissed the tousled top of his head. "Good night, Jean-Paul. Sleep tight."

She paused at the door, looking back at the cosy little scene. Agathe was in the armchair, sewing carefully. The two children were little rounded humps in their beds. The room was quiet, peaceful, comforting.

She sighed and went downstairs to dinner. She did not look forward to the evening ahead.

The dinner began quietly enough. Madame and Monsieur Treboul looked a little askance at Tony, but they were polite to him, and Louis's frigid silence went almost unnoticed. Marise was discreetly gowned in a stiff dark blue brocade, enriched by a collar of sparkling diamanté, her slim throat rising proudly, the sleek sweep of her black hair crowned by a butterfly of silver filigree. She looked so much the mistress of the house that Claire felt a grim misery seeping through her veins.

Tony, still casually dressed but wearing a tie for the occasion, could hardly keep his eyes from Marise.

He ate and drank in a daze, staring at her with hard, blue, hungry eyes.

Claire was not hungry, but her attempt to leave most of her plate untouched brought down upon her one of Louis's stern frowns, and she hurriedly picked a little, turning pale.

Clearly, Louis was extremely angry. He sat, very dark-visaged and brooding, raising his wine glass to his lips, the piercing grey eyes moving over the rim of the crystal to contemplate the other people at the table, his expression leaving little doubt that he was far from enjoying their company.

Madame leant over and asked Claire which season she thought the best for visiting Cornwall.

Flushing a little, as all eyes came to rest on her, Claire said that she herself preferred the late spring.

Madame nodded. "Spring is a wise time to travel," she agreed. "One gets fewer fellow travellers. And it is not too hot nor too cold." She smiled at Claire gently. "Then next spring we shall bring the children to visit Trevillion, *ma petite*!"

Claire was overjoyed. "Ah, thank you, *madame*. My father will be so happy! Even if he does marry again he'll want to see them."

"Marry again?" Louis leaned forward sharply, staring at her. "Your father plans to marry again? You did not mention this before."

Claire met his eyes, steeling herself to bear that sharp grey gaze. "Annette thinks my father may marry our next-door neighbour, Mrs. Dillon. I don't know if her suspicion is correct."

Louis's lean features tightened, his eyes probed hers.

"So? Dillon . . . this is the mother of your friend Peter Dillon?" He laid his palms flat on the damask tablecloth, his head thrust forward demandingly. "This is what disturbed you? This was the news your sister brought?"

She nodded dumbly.

He considered it for a moment. "I find that very strange," he said at last.

Marise, restless because Claire was engrossing his attention, laughed. "Why is it strange, *mon cher*? Surely Claire's father is not too old to marry again?"

He flicked her a curiously aloof glance. "It is not that," he said, then changed the subject by asking Tony which houses he had visited so far.

Tony talked lightly and easily, his rakish good looks at some disadvantage, in Claire's opinion, by contrast with Louis.

When they had finished dinner, they withdrew to the little salon for coffee as before, but Louis was restless, and when Monsieur and Madame Treboul pleaded weariness and left for bed, he put on the stereophonic radiogram which was concealed in an alcove behind glossily painted panelling.

The music whispered out, nostalgic and sweet, and Tony grinned at Marise.

"We could dance to this," he said casually.

She gave Louis a half nervous glance. He was standing with his back to them, staring at a small table on which stood a gilded crystal bowl.

"What do you think, Louis? Could we dance?" Marise laughed and touched his arm.

He flicked round, frowning, then said, "Dance?

Why, naturally, my dear Marise. But there is little room in here. . . ."

"It's a warm night," said Tony cheerfully. "We could open the french window and dance out along the terrace. It would be rather romantic! I bet they used to do it in the eighteenth century."

Louis looked at him oddly. "Yes, indeed they did," he agreed. "They hung coloured lanterns in the trees and danced and walked under the moon, while musicians sat in this room and played for them."

Tony grinned. "There you are, then! A good example to follow, don't you think?"

Louis went to the long window, pushed it open and looked out. A draught of sweet, warm air moved the curtains.

"Why not?" he murmured.

Tony held out a hand to Marise. She looked at him, her dark eyes blank, then turned her head slowly and looked at Louis. He was standing beside the radiogram, turning the sound up a little.

Tony slid his hand around Marise, his face close to hers, the brilliant blue eyes half laughing, half pleading.

He swayed gently to the music, and Marise sighed, and let herself move with him. They swirled around the room together, avoiding the furniture, and then Tony had lifted her out through the french windows into the darkness beyond. Claire had a glimpse of Marise, her smooth olive-skinned face set in a sort of bitter-sweet pleasure, the lids drawn down over the black eyes. Then they vanished.

She folded her hands in her lap, feeling acutely

embarrassed. Louis still stood with his back to her, fiddling with the radiogram. Was he unaware of the fact that Tony and Marise were dancing? Why did he stand there so stiffly, his shoulders squared as though tensed against pain?

She looked across the room at the curtains, blowing gently in the summer breeze. Her ears suddenly picked up a small movement, and she turned and saw Louis facing her, his eyes almost black with some concealed emotion.

"Why did Annette lie to me about this Peter Dillon?" he demanded. "Why should she do such a thing?"

Claire lifted helpless shoulders. "I . . . I don't know. . . ."

He came towards her, lifting her from the chair with cruel, determined hands, the long fingers digging into her arms. She looked up, with a sickening jolt of the heart, into a face almost unrecognisably savage.

"I found your sister hard and selfish," he said harshly. "Why do you permit people to use you as she and your father have used you? Have you no instinct for self-defence? You are too vulnerable, too easily touched into response. You weep for the little Marie-Claire, you weep for Madame Treboul. You were even ready to be sorry for the idle Tony Kirk, and Léon Frautbois, who is twice as capable of looking after himself as you are. . . . I watch you with these worthless people, pouring out your sweetness and compassion on them, and I feel a rage I cannot control!"

She was trembling, only held on her feet by the brutal grip of his hands.

"I'm sorry if I made you angry," she said falteringly.

He let out a long, furious breath. "You are sorry! You have submitted me to days of torture and uncertainty, and you look at me with those mild eyes and say you are sorry!" He shook her violently, bending over her with hot dark eyes. "It seems strange to me that although you expend so much emotion on others, you have none at all to spare for me! Am I not entitled to some of this compassion?"

Claire was dazed and bewildered, her eyes staring into the grey ones so close to her, trying to read the expression which made them almost black with rage. "What do you mean, Louis?"

"What do I mean?" He groaned. "This, Claire...." And his mouth seized hers demandingly, stinging her into incredulous, ecstatic life.

His hands slid down to her waist, moved up her back, gripping, hurting, delighting her. She was unable to disguise her response. Her body seemed to melt, to lean against him, her hands clung to his neck, touching the dark hair shyly.

He drew back, looking down with eyes that blazed. "I love you," he breathed.

She gave a soft cry and buried her face in his shoulder. His arms tightened until they hurt, but she could bear any pain in this moment.

He kissed her hair, her ear, murmured, "I have wanted this from the first moment I saw you. Everything Paul told me about you attracted me. I used to look at those photographs and envy the young man who was with you. Then when I saw you in the hotel, so shy and nervous, with your silky hair falling over your eyes, I felt a qualm somewhere inside me. From that moment I knew I had to have you." He brushed his lips against the curve of her cheek.

Claire listened intently, still hiding her face, trying to believe what he said.

"You cannot conceive my jealousy," he said, laughing a little. "I could hardly bear to see you with another man. I suspected everyone who looked at you. You were so hostile to me, so kind to everyone else. I was very afraid that I would lose you."

She moved protestingly against him, and he pulled her nearer. "Yes, my darling, I was like a man in torment. I did everything I could to keep others away from you. You were like a precious, fragile work of art. I was terrified a thief would make off with you!"

She looked up at him, her hands on his shoulders. "I think I loved you, too, from our first meeting, but I was confused by feeling so out of place at St. Hilaire. I was too conscious of my country upbringing. I felt that everyone was laughing at me."

He kissed her nose. "That timidity of yours must end, *ma chère*. You are Claire and you are beautiful. If you had read my thoughts you would have known the wonder I felt. I was even jealous of poor little Marie-Claire! She got your kisses and your loving tears. I got nothing but cold words and hard looks."

"No," she protested, shaking her head and laughing.

"But yes," he insisted. "You resented me from the start, as the owner of the hotel and a Frenchman. But now that your family problem is resolved we shall be able to do much for Paul's children. You will stay near them and see them often, and they will have little cousins to play with!"

She blushed hotly and he laughed aloud, joyful and triumphant.

Then Claire remembered Marise, and looked at him carefully. "Louis, what about Marise? I thought you were going to marry her?"

He looked surprised. "Marry Marise? *Ciel*, what gave you that idea? I have known her for most of her life. If I had wanted to marry her, I would have done so long ago! In any case, Marise has been involved with this Tony Kirk for some months. She really loves him, I am afraid, although I suspect it is much against her will. She knows what a wastrel he is, but. . . ." he shrugged. "That is why I was so afraid that you, too, would fall for him. He is a persuasive scoundrel."

Claire was thoughtful. So Louis had known about Tony and Marise! Poor Marise, her ambition to marry Louis had never been remotely likely, after all. She had sacrificed Tony for nothing. Claire could hardly tell Louis how she had got the impression that he would marry Marise. It would be best to say nothing more. Marise would have her pride intact, and knowing her, Claire knew that would be important to her.

Louis was looking at the open french window. "They have been out there a long time. I think we should discreetly withdraw, Claire!" He looked at her teasingly. "We have much to say to each other, and it must be said in private. We will go to my study where we will not be disturbed." He grinned down at her. "I can find it in my heart to be tolerant of Kirk, now. Marise might even reform him, who knows? We will leave them alone, anyway."

Claire let him lead her out of the room, his arm about her waist. She was still a little incredulous. Louis loved her. She repeated it silently to herself. Louis loved her. It was a little private miracle, just for her.

16 GREAT RE-ISSUES

Here is a wonderful opportunity to read many of the Harlequin Romances you may have missed.

- [ ] 917 TIMBER MAN
  Joyce Dingwell
- [ ] 920 MAN AT MULERA
  Kathryn Blair
- [ ] 926 MOUNTAIN MAGIC
  Susan Barrie
- [ ] 944 WHISPER OF DOUBT
  Andrea Blake
- [ ] 973 TIME OF GRACE
  Sara Seale
- [ ] 976 FLAMINGOS ON THE LAKE
  Isobel Chace
- [ ] 980 A SONG BEGINS
  Mary Burchell
- [ ] 992 SNARE THE WILD HEART
  Elizabeth Hoy

- [ ] 996 PERCHANCE TO MARY
  Celine Conway
- [ ] 997 CASTLE THUNDERBIRD
  Susan Barrie
- [ ] 999 GREEN FINGERS FARM
  Joyce Dingwell
- [ ] 1014 HOUSE OF LORRAINE
  Rachel Lindsey
- [ ] 1027 THE LONELY SHORE
  Anne Weale
- [ ] 1223 THE GARDEN OF PERSEPHON
  Nan Asquith
- [ ] 1245 THE BAY OF MOONLIGHT
  Rose Burghley
- [ ] 1319 BRITTLE BONDAGE
  Rosalind Brett

To: **HARLEQUIN READER SERVICE, Dept. N 401**
M.P.O. Box 707, Niagara Falls, N.Y. 14302
Canadian address: Stratford, Ont., Canada

- [ ] Please send me the free Harlequin Romance Catalogue.
- [ ] Please send me the titles checked.

I enclose $_____ (No C.O.D.'s), All books are 60c each. To help defray postage and handling cost, please add 25c.

Name _____

Address _____

City/Town _____

State/Prov. _____ Zip _____

FREE! *Harlequin Romance Catalogue*

Here is a wonderful opportunity to read many of the Harlequin Romances you may have missed.

The HARLEQUIN ROMANCE CATALOGUE lists hundreds of titles which possibly are no longer available at your local bookseller. To receive your copy, just fill out the coupon below, mail it to us, and we'll rush your catalogue to you!

Following this page you'll find a sampling of a few of the Harlequin Romances listed in the catalogue. Should you wish to order any of these immediately, kindly check the titles desired and mail with coupon.

To: **HARLEQUIN READER SERVICE, Dept. N 401**
M.P.O. Box 707, Niagara Falls, N.Y. 14302
Canadian address: Stratford, Ont., Canada

☐ Please send me the free Harlequin Romance Catalogue.

☐ Please send me the titles checked.

I enclose $_____ (No C.O.D.'s), All books are 60c each. To help defray postage and handling cost, please add 25c.

Name _____

Address _____

City/Town _____

State/Prov. _____ Zip_____

Have You Missed Any of These
Harlequin Romances?

☐ 748 THE VALLEY OF PALMS
      Jean S. MacLeod
☐ 772 CHLOE WILDE, STUDENT
      NURSE, Joan Turner
☐ 793 THE STARCHED CAP
      Valerie K. Nelson
☐ 820 THE WORLD OF NURSE
      MITCHELL, H. Nickson
☐ 892 THE HOUSE OF THE
      SWALLOWS, J. Armstrong
☐ 907 TWO FOR THE DOCTOR
      Joan Blair
☐ 916 DOCTOR VANNARD'S
      PATIENTS, Pauline Ash
☐ 945 DOCTOR SANDY
      Margaret Malcolm
☐ 965 CAME A STRANGER
      Celine Conway
☐ 967 THE WINGS OF THE
      MORNING, Susan Barrie
☐ 989 HOTEL MIRADOR
      Rosalind Brett
☐ 1046 THREE WOMEN
      Celine Conway
☐ 1054 MY TENDER FURY
      Margaret Malcolm
☐ 1059 THE TULIP TREE
      Kathryn Blair
☐ 1060 HUNTSMAN'S FOLLY
      Alex Stuart
☐ 1086 GAY CAVALIER
      Alex Stuart
☐ 1089 HOSPITAL BY THE LAKE
      Anne Durham
☐ 1092 THE SOUND OF GUITARS
      Jill Tahourdin
☐ 1099 CARPET OF DREAMS
      Susan Barrie
☐ 1129 MY FRIEND, DOCTOR JOHN
      Marjorie Norrell
☐ 1133 WISH ON A STAR
      Patricia Fenwick
☐ 1137 DOCTOR AT DRUMLOCHAN
      Iris Danbury
☐ 1138 LOVING IS GIVING
      Mary Burchell
☐ 1139 THE HOUSE OF MY ENEMY
      Norrey Ford
☐ 1153 THE RETURN OF SISTER
      BARNETT, E. Houghton

☐ 1155 MISS MIRANDA'S WALK
      Betty Beaty
☐ 1159 THE GAY GORDONS
      Barbara Allen
☐ 1193 HOSPITAL IN KASHMIR
      Belinda Dell
☐ 1198 HAPPY EVER AFTER
      Dorothy Rivers
☐ 1204 THIS WAS LOVE
      Jean Curtis
☐ 1213 THE MOONFLOWER
      Jean S. Macleod
☐ 1232 A DAY LIKE SPRING
      Jane Fraser
☐ 1233 A LOVE OF HER OWN
      Hilda Pressley
☐ 1236 JEMIMA   Leonora Starr
☐ 1270 THOUGH WORLDS APART
      Mary Burchell
☐ 1272 DEVON INTERLUDE
      Kay Thorpe
☐ 1275 SHAKE OUT THE STARS
      Janice Gray
☐ 1282 THE SHINING STAR
      Hilary Wilde
☐ 1284 ONLY MY HEART TO GIVE
      Nan Asquith
☐ 1285 OUT OF A DREAM
      Jean Curtis
☐ 1286 BE MORE THAN DREAMS
      Elizabeth Hoy
☐ 1312 PEPPERCORN HARVEST
      Ivy Ferrari
☐ 1313 MANN OF THE MEDICAL
      WING, Ann Durham
☐ 1322 WIND THROUGH THE
      VINEYARDS, J. Armstrong
☐ 1337 THE CAMPBELLS ARE
      COMING. Felicity Hayle
☐ 1352 THE MOUNTAIN OF STARS
      Catherine Airlie
☐ 1358 HOME TO WHITE WINGS
      Jean Dunbar
☐ 1359 RETURN TO TREMARTH
      Susan Barrie
☐ 1369 NURSE RONA CAME TO
      ROTHMERE, Louise Ellis
☐ 1372 ISLE OF POMEGRANATES
      Iris Danbury
☐ 1374 FORTUNE'S LEAD
      Barbara Perkins

All books are 60c. Please use the handy order coupon.